After all these y~~~~
moon and hung~~~~
home. A man now. A gorgeous man. But still
Tony.

He looked so different from the skinny boy she'd shadowed as a little girl. The boy who had awakened feelings too powerful to deny that day in the tree house. The day she'd told him she loved him.

The next day, he was gone.

This was the guy who'd shattered her tender heart when he'd abandoned Noah's Crossing, his nonna and her.

But he'd finally come home to make things right with his nonna. As for making things right with *her*?

It was far too late for that.

She pressed her hand to the stab in her heart. *How can I possibly forgive him for that lonely, frozen morning when I had to give away our precious baby girl?*

Books by Carol Voss

Love Inspired

Love of a Lifetime
Instant Daddy

CAROL VOSS

Always an avid reader with a vivid imagination, Carol grew up in Smalltown, Wisconsin, with church ice-cream socials, Fourth of July parades, summer carnivals and people knowing and caring about everybody else. What better backdrop for heroes and heroines to fall in love?

In the years between business college and a liberal arts degree, Carol worked in a variety of businesses, married, raised two sons and a daughter and did volunteer work for church, school, Scouts, 4-H and hospice. She is an award-winning author of family stories.

Carol lives near Madison, Wisconsin, with her creative husband, her sweet, vibrating border collie and her supervisory cat. Besides writing, she loves reading, walking her dog, biking, flower gardening, traveling and, most of all, God, home and family. She loves to hear from readers at carol@carolvoss.com.

Love of a Lifetime
Carol Voss

Love Inspired

Recycling programs
for this product may
not exist in your area.

LOVE INSPIRED BOOKS

ISBN-13: 978-0-373-87738-6

LOVE OF A LIFETIME

www.LoveInspiredBooks.com

Printed in U.S.A.

For if you forgive men when they sin against you,
your heavenly Father will also forgive you.
—*Matthew* 6:14

To Emily and Melissa
for their confidence and thoughtful suggestions.
To Ann for making the writing journey so much fun.

And to Gil and my fantastic family
for their constant love and support.

Chapter One

He'd prayed all the way from Brazil to northwestern Wisconsin for God to spare his nonna, even when God and he both knew his prayer was a selfish one.

Warm wind buffeting him, Tony Stefano leaned the Harley into the big curve and braced for his first glimpse of Nonna's Victorian in ten years. He roared round the corner, and there it stood. Tall. Proud. Unbending.

Like his nonna.

A lump caught in his throat. He felt just like he had when he'd left at seventeen…trapped in circumstances he had no clue how to handle. Nonna's demands. His overwhelming feelings for Maggie McGuire. And the final straw…Sheriff Bunker's accusations.

He gave his head a shake as if he could shake off the past and focused on the crisis at hand. According to Maggie's brief email, Nonna had fallen down the stairs and injured her leg and who knew what else. A shock. Somehow he'd thought his grandmother would live forever.

He had to see her one last time. He needed to ask her forgiveness before she went to meet her maker.

Gut churning, he took the turn into the driveway. Tires popped gravel. He braked to a stop beside the polished gray-and-white Suburban Maggie's dad had let him drive a few times. He couldn't believe she still had it. It must be a classic by now.

Hitting the kill switch on the Harley, he lifted off his helmet and squinted up at the sagging roof of the old house. Chipped paint and rotting windowsills. Keeping up a big, old house was like pouring money down a hole. But Nonna had always kept the place looking good with little cash, plenty of hard work and sheer determination. By the looks of it now, she was running low on all three.

Why hadn't she cashed those checks he'd sent?

At least her flowers were going stronger than ever. The place was draped in them, the air sweet with a fragrance that reminded him of Maggie. She'd loved Nonna's flowers, especially the roses. He peered through hundreds of pink ones climbing the arched arbor over the brick walk and caught a glimpse of copper hair.

Maggie.

His jaw clenched down on feelings he'd buried long ago. But he couldn't deny seeing her again filled him with anticipation mixed with…sheer terror. Pretty much the way she'd affected him ever since he'd hit town when he was six, and she'd been four. He climbed off the bike and ducked through the roses.

She stood near the back steps, hammer in hand, boards helter-skelter around her bare feet, a yellow T-shirt and worn, torn jeans skimming her curves.

He should have guessed she'd grow into a striking woman with those new-penny curls and big, brown eyes. Eyes filled with trust and belief in him those years growing up when they were the only kids for miles. Innocent eyes that had reminded him of his protective side.

Except for the day he'd betrayed her trust and taken her innocence. Sure, he'd been a head-over-heels-in-love kid of seventeen, but she'd been only fifteen. He'd asked God's forgiveness, but he doubted he'd ever forgive himself.

"Tony?" Maggie squinted at him as if she couldn't be sure who he was. "You came home?"

"I started out as soon as I got your email." Stopping in front of her, he tried to prepare for an answer to the question he feared asking. "How's Nonna?"

"She's slowly improving. The hospital in Eau Claire transferred her to the new rehab center on the other end of town yesterday."

Relief flooding him, he breathed a silent thank-you and grinned. "That's great news."

A frown flitted across Maggie's face. "She's very unhappy. She expected to come straight home from the hospital." She brightened a little. "But seeing you will cheer her up."

He hoped so. Now all he had to do was figure out what to say to her. "I need to set things right with her."

"It's about time." Maggie's face crumpling, she reached for him. "I'm so glad you came home to see her."

He swept her into a bear hug, her fresh scent touting hours outdoors. Memories of innocent kisses popped into his mind. Did she still taste like strawberries?

She pushed away, swiping at her eyes, a soft pink tinge flushing her cheeks and neck.

She was blushing?

"Your nonna's missed you so much."

What about you, Maggie? Have you missed me? Had she thought about him like he'd thought about her?

But they weren't kids anymore. They'd both moved on with their lives. His chest aching somewhere in the vicinity of his heart, he noticed a few freckles still spattered her nose. For some reason, he was glad they hadn't all disappeared.

She glanced at her watch. "It's nearly six. Your nonna goes to sleep early, but if you hurry, you can probably see her before she goes to sleep for the night."

He rubbed the back of his neck. "Nonna was always a stickler for cleanliness, so I should probably get cleaned up first. I've spent the last twenty hours on planes, in airports or eating truck exhaust. I'd kill for a shower."

"You don't have time. Splash water on your face." Maggie at her all-business best.

He frowned. "I don't know what to say to her."

"Just talk." She waved her hand as if to point out the obvious.

Unfortunately, God hadn't given everybody Maggie's talent for rebuilding bridges with people. "What can I say to her?"

She squinted. "There will probably be apologizing involved. Tell her you're sorry for running away."

"I have a feeling sorry is not going to cut it."

"It's a place to start."

He'd like to believe it was that simple, but... He dug deeper for words to make Maggie understand. "I figure raising a six-year-old kid after his mother died couldn't have been a piece of cake. Especially one with a chip on his shoulder the size of South America. I owe her. Big-time."

"Yes, you do."

"But you know nothing was ever easy between Nonna and me."

"She loves you, Tony." Her smile softened the intensity of that statement.

"You sure?"

"Of course I'm sure. She'll be so glad to see you… but it might take a while for her to forgive you. For running away. And for never coming home."

He dragged in a breath. "What about you, Maggie? Have you forgiven me for running away?"

"Me?" She stared at his boots. "Ten years is a long time."

Which meant no, she hadn't forgiven him and probably never would. But could he blame her?

"Stella keeps your letters stashed in the chest in her room. We—" Frowning, Maggie shook her head. "She rereads them so often, they're falling apart."

"That's hard to believe."

"Well, it's true. Just how long are you planning to stay?"

"I have to be on a plane for Porto Loges in a week."

"A week?" She gave him a scouring look.

"Can't be helped. We're starting a building contract I've worked hard to get off the ground."

"And *they* need you more than your nonna does?"

"I have a great foreman, but so many things go wrong, especially in the beginning of a project. Besides—Nonna has never needed me, and you know it."

Shaking her head, Maggie raised her chin a notch, a move that had always put him on his guard.

It worked as effectively as it always had. She clearly thought he was making excuses. "I have a lot to lose, Maggie. I need to get back to keep my financial backers from getting nervous."

She sighed. "And you think you can make up for ten years in a week?"

A tall order, he knew. He rubbed his whisker-stubbled chin and realized he didn't even know how to begin with Nonna. He needed to take Maggie with him. Just like old times. Him needing her help. But what else was he going to do? "Will you help me with Nonna?"

She frowned. "What makes you think I can help?"

"You've known us a long time. You can steer us around our old hang-ups."

"I had no idea I held such power."

He gave her a look. "Will you come with me?"

"It will be better if you see her alone."

Not a good plan. "We haven't seen each other for ten years."

"I can't go with you. She doesn't know I wrote to you. She needs to believe coming home was *your* idea."

Leave it to Maggie to overthink this. He shifted his stance. "Coming back *was* my idea. And I really need your help. Who else am I going to ask?"

She frowned.

But she hadn't said no. Not yet anyway. "You think my being here will help her, right?"

"Seeing you will give her a huge boost."

"Not if we get off on the wrong foot."

She narrowed her eyes as if giving his comment serious thought. "It'll take a couple minutes for me to change clothes."

He grinned his thanks. "I owe you."

"I'll remember that." She laid down her hammer and jogged up the porch steps, the screen door slamming shut behind her.

Her absence giving him time to think about what lay ahead, he stood there fighting a wave of panic. Pretty ridiculous. He was going to face his grandmother, not a firing squad.

Too bad he couldn't shake the feeling that the firing squad would be easier.

In her upstairs bedroom, Maggie pulled on clean jeans with shaking hands.

He was home.

After all these years, the boy who'd lit the moon and hung the stars in her sky was home. A man now. A gorgeous man. But still Tony.

And he was more. More rugged. More confident. More exciting. More everything she didn't need in her life.

He looked so different from the skinny boy she'd shadowed as a little girl. The boy who'd been her protector, her confidant, her friend. The boy whose kisses had awakened feelings too powerful to deny that day years ago. The day she'd told him she loved him.

She glanced at the chest beside her bed, her gaze skimming the princess figurine her parents had given her and homing in on the gold, oval locket draping its neck. Tony had given her the locket that day, a present for her fifteenth birthday.

The next day, he was gone.

Instead, Sheriff Bunker had shown up on her doorstep asking questions and accusing Tony of hurting Doc Tilbert and stealing his money. He did errands and odd jobs for the doctor, but Tony would never hurt him or steal from anybody. That's what she'd told the sheriff, but he was convinced Tony ran away because he was guilty, and vowed to send bulletins to surrounding law-enforcement agencies to find him. She'd been so afraid for Tony.

She grabbed her pink T-shirt from the bed and threw it over her head, jabbing blindly for the sleeves. Finally, she got the shirt on and dragged in a breath.

She was so relieved Tony had come home to see Stella that she hadn't given any thought to what it would be like having him around. Now it was all she could think about, and she couldn't stop shaking. In some ways, she felt like that same giddy schoolgirl all over again. How silly. How humiliating. How dumb.

This was the guy who'd shattered her heart when he'd abandoned Noah's Crossing, his nonna and her. The guy who'd jotted a postcard to his nonna to let her know he was okay, then dropped off the face of the earth for five years. The one who hated the town she considered home, who had no use for roots and couldn't wait to leave it all behind again.

But he'd finally come home to make things right with his nonna. Part of her couldn't help being proud of him for that. As for making things right with *her?*

It was far too late for that.

She pressed her hand to the stab in her heart and lowered herself to the bed. *Dear God, I thought I'd forgiven him for deserting me when I needed him most. But seeing him again, I know I haven't. Our baby isn't coming back—she's gone forever.*

Chapter Two

Tony splashed his face with water at Nonna's ancient kitchen sink, then attempted to keep his mind off his meeting with Nonna by stacking Maggie's boards against the porch railing to prevent her from tripping over them.

Hearing her swing through the door onto the porch, he straightened to look at her and couldn't help grinning. "Looking good, Magnolia Blossom."

She rolled her eyes heavenward. "Nobody calls me that."

He chuckled. Ten years, and he still liked teasing her.

"Thanks for stacking the boards."

"You're welcome. What are they for?"

"I'm building a ramp, but all I have so far are slivers and lots of bent nails."

He stacked the last board. "Sounds like a problem. But a ramp? You think Nonna will make it home?"

She clamped her eyes closed for a moment as if she didn't want to face any other possibility. "She'll probably need a wheelchair or walker at first."

"Is that what her doctors say?"

"Doctors don't know everything."

"Maybe not. But even if you do get her in the house, how's she going to deal with a wheelchair or walker when, I assume, the only bathroom is still upstairs?"

"I'm going to hire a carpenter to tear out the pantry and put in a downstairs bathroom. I would have done it already if Stella would have let the carpenter in the door."

Looked like Maggie needed a dose of reality. "This place could use more than a ramp and a downstairs bathroom. There's no sense putting good money into it if it isn't sound."

"Of course it's sound. It needs fresh paint and a few repairs, but it's still a magnificent house."

"You're living in the past, Blossom. Maybe it was magnificent once, but no more." He gestured up at the house. "Look at the way that roof sags. There's more wrong than peeling paint and rotting gingerbread. Repairs and updating costs could be astronomical."

"Money is not the point. Stella's survival is."

He turned her words over in his mind, trying to make sense of them. "Well…money *is* a consideration. And I can afford a nursing home or assisted-living facility for her."

"With no gardens? She'd hate it."

"Maybe at first, but she'd get used to it."

Maggie shook her head. "You *still* haven't figured out how important home and roots are to your nonna?"

"That's not the issue—"

"Yes, it is. Her home and gardens are more than a house and a piece of land to her, Tony. This is the place that nourishes her soul."

A muscle in his jaw jumped. "Things change, Maggie. Even in Noah's Crossing. You have to see that Nonna's situation has changed."

"It doesn't have to change. Her whole life is here. It's all she has left of your grandfather Salvatore. She's lived here for sixty years. She wants to live out her days here."

"Maybe she does, but she has to be practical. And so do you."

"This from a man who lives in the Brazilian rain forest?" She threw her hands in the air, a gesture he remembered well. "I have *always* been practical."

"Compared to what?"

"What's that supposed to mean?"

"Sounds to me like you're still the idealist you were when we were kids. You had more bright ideas to set the world right than I could keep up with. We raised money to save whales, wild mustangs, feral cats—"

"Didn't I carry out my ideas?"

He shrugged. "Well, sure…but…idealist or not, you must see this house isn't a safe place for Nonna. Maybe she'll even need professional care."

"If she does, we'll find in-home care." Maggie bit her lip. "She needs to come home, Tony. If she has that to hang on to, she'll fight to get well."

He scraped his fingers through his hair. "Things never stay the same, Maggie. No matter how hard you try to hang on to them."

She narrowed her eyes, looking ready to draw blood. "And running away never solves a thing, Tony."

"Touché," he mumbled. Apparently, little Magnolia Blossom had learned how to wound. He didn't like thinking he'd probably taught her that.

Glancing at her watch, she headed for the driveway. "If you're leaving in a week, we don't have a minute to lose."

He strode to the Harley. "I'll have us there in no time."

She held up her keys. "I'm not in the mood to take my life in my hands."

"You'd be perfectly safe. Must be all of two miles." He held his helmet out to her. "Wear this."

She glared at the helmet and shook her head.

He looked down his nose. "Please don't tell me you've turned into a sissy since I left."

She opened her mouth as if to deny his accusation, then shut it. Glowering at him, she jerked the helmet from his hand. "I am *not* a sissy."

Five minutes later, they roared for town on the Harley, Maggie clinging to Tony's back like a terrified monkey. Maybe teasing her about turning into a sissy hadn't been the nicest thing to do, but it was uncanny how quickly old habits were asserting themselves. Hadn't he always used teasing to avoid confrontation with her?

His immediate problem, though, was that she was a strong woman with a grip to match, and if he didn't get oxygen soon, he was going to black out. "You have to let me breathe," he yelled over the roar of the bike.

"Sorry."

He didn't so much hear the word as feel it. She loosened her grip a bit, but he could still feel her arms hugging his middle, a welcome distraction to worrying about facing Nonna. "Lean with me in the turns and keep your feet on the pegs. You'll be fine."

"I like more steel between me and the pavement," she yelled.

"The Hog gets a whole lot better gas mileage than that bus of yours."

"What about comfort?"

"You're uncomfortable?" He could feel her groan. He chuckled.

The countryside opened up to pastures and patches of tall hickories and scraggy bur oaks intermingled with birches and pines. Northern Wisconsin still had an unspoiled beauty about it.

Thundering around a bend, he scowled at the upscale new houses sprawling over Doc Tilbert's land. Asphalt roads and culs-de-sac cut into the woods he and Maggie had roamed with his golden retriever. So much for unspoiled.

Finally, he downshifted as they rode into town.

A young couple with ice-cream cones strolled hand in hand along the sidewalk. An older man strove to keep up with his giant schnauzer. Several teenage boys rode bikes along the street, probably looking for something to do. He wished them luck with that.

With the scent of fried onions wafting past his nose, Tony caught a glimpse of the squad car parked in front of Jessie's Main Street Diner and downshifted again. If Bunker was still sheriff, no point in alerting him that Tony was back, even if Nonna had written that Danny Judd had ultimately been arrested for that robbery.

Familiar houses crowded the sidewalk. He'd once known who lived in every one of those houses. Now, most sported fresh paint, and some displayed shop signs. The Chocolate Nugget, The Knit and Pearl, Grampa's Workshop.

It would take a lot more than paint and a few quaint signs to change this town. No doubt, the tourist-friendly facade still hid too many people who judged first and asked questions later. People just like Sheriff Bunker.

Loosening her stranglehold round his waist, Maggie shifted her weight.

What? She was waving to somebody? He glanced around, noting a middle-aged couple waving back. He sure didn't need an old-home parade down Main Street. He hunkered down and tried to ignore people who, no doubt, were trying to figure out who he was. But maybe nobody knew who Maggie was either in that helmet.

"Hi, Maggie," somebody yelled.

There went that hope. He notched up the speed a little and focused straight ahead. Reaching the other end of town, he spotted a sign announcing the Pleasant View Rehabilitation Center and smoothly turned into the parking lot. He pulled to a stop, braced the bike with his feet and let the engine idle for no good reason. Unless his subconscious was looking for a quick getaway. Not a bad idea, but having come all this way, its timing was off. He killed the motor.

"We made it." Maggie sat there as if digesting that fact.

He pushed his sunglasses up on his head. "See? Perfectly safe."

She crawled off the bike and handed him his helmet.

He hung it on the handlebar and dismounted, giving the low-slung, new building a once-over. Sound structure with shutters and a few details lending a homey feel without budget-eating extras. Obviously, a practical architect. Good for him. Or her.

"Tony, promise me you won't say anything to upset Stella."

He frowned. "Why would I want to do that?"

"Nothing about living someplace other than her house. Promise me." The look in her eyes said she was in a no-nonsense mood.

"Fine, I promise." Heaving a fortifying breath, he entered the rehab center with Maggie at his side, her fresh scent as mysterious as a rain forest. Too bad he didn't have time to dwell on that instead of the eerily quiet tiled hall and the medicinal smell with floral undertones. Not like a funeral home smelled, but close enough.

"Relax," Maggie instructed.

"Easy for you to say."

"You'll be fine."

He was an idiot. *And* a coward. Nonna was somewhere close to eighty years old and injured. And he needed to improve his attitude before he faced her. He wasn't a kid anymore. He could do this.

"Here we are." Maggie stopped at a doorway. "You go in first."

He raised a brow.

"I'm right behind you."

With a sigh, he walked in. So this was what a standard room in a rehab center looked like. Not too bad. The room was filled with natural light from a large window overlooking tranquil farm fields. A vase of flowers sat on the wide window ledge anchoring a display of get-well cards and a few framed pictures of people and flowers. A clock hung over a bulletin board proclaiming the date and day of the week.

Finally, he brought his gaze to the bed. Nonna leaned against pillows, her eyes closed. He cringed at the multicolored bruises covering her weathered face and arms. She looked so old and fragile and helpless that it was hard to comprehend this woman was his strong, proud nonna who'd never needed anyone. Especially him.

Maggie took his arm and guided him over to the bed. She bent and kissed Nonna's wrinkled cheek, Maggie's health and vitality almost shocking in contrast to his grandmother's. "Are you asleep?"

"Only resting." Nonna opened her eyes to look at Maggie, a softness in her expression Tony didn't remember.

Maggie stepped back and urged him closer to Nonna.

Nonna frowned up at him as if she wasn't sure she could trust her eyes. "Anthony?"

"How are you doing?" He bent low. Should he kiss her? Had he ever kissed her when he was a kid? Or she him? She'd never been one of those soft, fuzzy grandmothers people talk about. Deciding to follow Maggie's lead, he kissed Nonna's cheek and straightened. There. That hadn't been so hard, had it?

Nonna gave him a serious once-over. "You have grown into a man."

"I have." He had to grin as he caught himself stretching a little taller.

"You are even more like your papa than you were as a boy."

Despite his best efforts, he stiffened.

As if sensing his dissent, Nonna narrowed her eyes. "Have you grown into a man inside as well as outside?"

"I try."

"Are you home to stay?"

Home. In the eleven years he'd lived with her, never once had he considered Noah's Crossing his home. But what was the point of telling her that again? "For a short time."

She narrowed her eyes accusingly.

Obviously, a subject change was needed. "You look awfully good for a woman who fell down a flight of stairs. How did that happen?"

She smoothed her bedsheet with arthritic fingers. "I was hungry."

"She went downstairs in the middle of the night to get a snack," Maggie supplied.

Nonna pursed her lips as if disgusted. "My knee acts up when I do not expect it."

"Thankfully, I woke up and found her." Maggie lovingly stroked Nonna's arm.

"I'm glad Maggie moved back with you after college." Even if, just like when he'd read Nonna's letter, he still couldn't figure out why Maggie had returned to Noah's Crossing once she'd escaped.

"Maggie is an angel." Nonna beamed at her.

Maggie clasped her hand. "I'm the fortunate one."

As Tony watched, their obvious love and respect for each other made him feel every bit the outsider he was, in spite of the Stefano blood pulsing through his arteries. "How long does the doctor think your hip will take to heal?"

Nonna gave a vague wave of her hand. "The doctor sees an old woman and thinks she is too old to mend."

"If you're not happy with your doctor, why don't you talk to another one?" he asked.

"Doctors cost money," she stated flatly.

"Use the checks I sent. I'll send more money. I'm working on a big building contract in South America now."

"South America is not your home, Anthony."

Not the home thing again. He'd never been anything but honest about his aversion for Noah's Crossing.

"He's home now." Maggie peered into Nonna's eyes. "You need to enjoy him while he's here."

Leave it to Maggie to inject a positive note. Good thing he'd convinced her to come with him.

"Anthony, your checks are in the cookie jar on the

second shelf in the pantry. You must use them to pay for my funeral."

Outspoken as always. "Who said anything about dying?"

Maggie gave him a stricken look and focused on Nonna. "Of course you're not going to die. Soon, your body will mend and you'll be home working in your gardens with me again."

Tony frowned at the certainty in her tone. She was living in a fantasy. Even if Nonna did recover, the old house had no accommodations for an elderly woman with a walker or a wheelchair.

"You will sleep in your old room, Anthony," Nonna said matter-of-factly.

The room where he'd spent sleepless nights hatching elaborate schemes to run away to join his dad? He'd probably have nightmares. "I'll stay at the motel near the rehabilitation center." He crooked his thumb in that direction.

Nonna scowled. "You must stay in your home with Maggie and Hannah and sleep in your room."

Didn't she understand he wasn't a kid she could order around anymore? He stole a glance urging Maggie to bail him out.

She didn't look any too happy with Nonna's command either. She glanced his way. "Just don't expect a spiffy house and down-home cooking," she said dryly.

No bailout there. This was turning into the nightmare he'd envisioned every time guilt had prodded him to come back. "I'm not used to either one. But who's Hannah?"

"She is the granddaughter of a good friend who moved to Eau Claire this winter," Nonna said, as if that explained everything.

It didn't. "Why is she living at your house?"

"She needed a job for the summer, and Della needed help in the diner."

"So you gave her a place to stay?"

"Of course."

So now Maggie was responsible for her? He glanced in her direction.

"Hannah keeps me company while Stella is mending," Maggie said.

"Of course," Tony answered, wondering just how high Maggie's stack of responsibilities went.

"You must not forget your home or your memories, Anthony. Memories remind us of our roots. Of who we are. Where we belong."

Back to the home theme? He turned to his nonna. "I came back to see *you,* not to dredge up memories."

"Dare I expect anything from my only grandchild?" Challenge blazed from the old woman's dark eyes.

He wanted to jab back. Apparently, old habits died hard. But she was elderly and injured, he reminded himself as he held on to reason. Every letter, every phone call, she urged him to come home. He studied her. "I came back to honor you."

Her eyes opened a little wider. "How can I believe you when you did not honor your own papa in his coffin?"

Aw, back to good old Dad again. Tony clenched his jaw hard, fighting to imprison harsh words. Why in the world would he have flown across several continents to honor the man who'd ditched him when he was six? But in this case, he had a good reason. "I didn't receive your letter in time. I phoned to tell you that."

"Tony, will you add water to the wildflowers on the window ledge?" Maggie's voice cut through the tension.

If anybody knew how he felt about his dad, it was Maggie, and she was obviously giving him an out.

"You must never forget your papa, Anthony."

She couldn't be serious. "He forgot *me* when I was six."

Maggie jerked her head to glare at him as if he'd done something unforgivable. Nonna's look felt even worse.

You'd think he was a kid again. "It's the truth," he said in his own defense.

"He could not take you with him on his violin tours," Nonna stated.

"Why not? I toured with him and my mother before she died."

Nonna looked away.

What was he doing? He negotiated with some very powerful people. Why did he have so much trouble carrying on a simple conversation with his grandmother? Remembering he was there because he owed her an apology or two, he tried to regroup. "I'm sorry I couldn't be here to help you in your grief."

"A good son would honor his papa."

Her words felt like a kick to the gut. "And a good father wouldn't abandon his kid."

Nonna glared at him. "He was a good papa before your mamma died."

"What about all those years after?"

"He did the best he could."

"No, he didn't. He dumped me and never came back, never even remembered my birthdays."

"He called on the telephone."

Tony had always suspected Nonna tracked down his father and insisted he talk to his son. "Only to make promises he never intended to keep. You can't defend that."

Maggie shoved the vase of flowers into his hand. "Get water for these."

He met her eyes and realized how far off the mark his reunion with Nonna had gone.

Maggie held his gaze, as if willing him to keep his mouth shut.

He grasped the vase. Chest heavy, he turned and headed for the door. Was making peace with Nonna too much to hope for?

"I'll be right back, Stella." Maggie fell into step beside him.

Out in the hall, he strode away from Nonna's room as fast as he could...even when what he really wanted was to charge back into the fray and make Nonna see her son for what he was. Why couldn't she understand his point for once and admit he'd had a rotten father?

"Hey, Tony," Maggie's voice interrupted. "The water for the flowers is in the other direction."

He stopped and turned to face her. "That sure went well."

She gave him a serious frown. "You promised you wouldn't upset her. She needs all her strength to heal."

"She attacked *me,* not the other way around."

"She's hurt because you've ignored her all these years. She misses you."

He eyed her incredulously. "Is that why she's so glad to see me?"

"She needs you, Tony. She's just too proud to admit it."

"Oh, come on. She doesn't need me any more than she ever did. What a joke to think I could fix things and put this place behind me once and for all."

Maggie took a step back, mouth open, eyes wide. She looked...stunned.

"What? You were there. Nonna and I still can't be in the same room without tearing into each other. Obviously, I don't know how to change that."

She gave him a pinched look, as if trying to decide how best to deal with him.

He *hated* being dealt with. He crammed the vase of flowers into her hand, turned on his heel and strode for the door.

"Where are you going?"

"Back to Brazil." He kept on walking.

She bolted in front of him and blocked his way, holding the vase of flowers out like a barrier.

He grasped her shoulders to keep from running her over.

"You can't march in and get her all upset, then leave. Instead of helping her, you'll only add to her problems. If you don't make this right, I'll never speak to you again." The set of her lips told him she meant it.

A sinking feeling hollowed out the pit of his stomach. Even after all these years, Maggie's opinion of him still mattered. A lot more than he wanted it to.

He especially hated that she was right.

He owed Nonna big-time. If she hadn't taken him in, he had no idea who his dad would have dumped him with when he'd had his fill of parenting. Sure, Tony had locked horns with her over just about everything, but she'd never turned her back on him. Without her, who knew what path his anger might have taken? What kind of man he'd be?

He'd come back to make things right with Nonna, but was that even possible? Maybe he should just make arrangements for her to live out her life in a comfortable, safe place, then leave.

But that wouldn't take care of the guilt that weighed him down like a sack of cement. If he left without giving his relationship with Nonna his best shot, he'd fail her, he'd fail Maggie and he'd fail himself. And he'd regret it for the rest of his life.

Didn't he already have more than his share of regrets?

Chapter Three

Nearing seven-thirty, Maggie walked into Jessie's Main Street Diner, very aware of Tony on her heels. How she would get through the week with him underfoot, she didn't know. It would be so much easier to let him leave, if she wasn't completely convinced Stella needed him.

And he needed Stella even if he hadn't figured that out yet. Whether he and his nonna could let go of their old arguments and find each other, she didn't know that either. But she did know she had to put aside her own feelings and try to help.

The familiar rattle of dishes boosted her spirits a tad, and she took a deep breath of mouthwatering aromas of fried burgers with onions, roast beef and her favorite, chicken potpie. At least, her growling stomach assured her that her light-headedness might have less to do with Tony and more to do with her forgetting to eat lunch.

A few people she knew sat at the long counter, probably having dessert because it was well past dinner hour. One of the new booths was occupied with a middle-aged couple she didn't know. Tourists, she guessed. She glanced at Tony. "What do you think of the changes to the diner?"

He frowned. "It's bigger."

"Della knocked out a wall or two."

"If this is Della's place, why is 'Jessie's Main Street Diner' on the sign out front?"

"Because Della sold it to Jessie, then Jess got married and moved to Madison. She's very happy, but I miss her like crazy. Anyway, Della bought back the diner, but she thought it would just be too confusing to change it back to Della's Diner."

"*More* confusing than it is now?" With a shake of his head, he grasped Maggie's elbow, guided her to a red booth and glumly settled opposite her.

Obviously, he was thinking about his disastrous meeting with Stella. He hadn't wanted to stop at the diner. Maggie had insisted, food only one of her reasons. She wanted to introduce him to Hannah. Besides, the diner was Noah's Crossing's communal living room. A place where people came to hear and share news as much as to eat, and everybody left feeling better than when they'd arrived.

Maggie could use some of that right now. And so could Tony, whether he acknowledged it or not. "Della's food is as good as ever. And her desserts are still unbelievable." Her mouth watered just thinking about the custard pie. "You won't be sorry I made you stop."

He gave a little grunt.

How had his meeting with his nonna gotten so completely out of hand? Things had been a little rocky from the start, but Maggie had never in a million years been ready for the rapid-fire explosion between them.

What can I do to help them, God?

While she left their problem in God's hands for the

moment, she supposed she could try to figure out how to cheer up Tony. Della's food would definitely help. "Well, I'm starved. And like I told you, I don't cook."

Tony studied the menu. "I do."

"Really?" she asked skeptically.

Eyeing Tony, the cute, chubby fifteen-year-old Hannah set two glasses of water on the table. "There's some chicken potpie left, Maggie."

"Fantastic. I'll have that with a salad and milk." She glanced at Tony. "Hannah, this is Tony, Mrs. Stefano's grandson. He's in town for a few days and will be living at the house with us."

Hannah stole a shy glance at Tony. Hannah was *not* normally shy.

But with the grumpy look on Tony's face, who could blame her? Obviously, he was still reviewing his exchanges with his nonna. "Do you know what you want, Tony?"

He jammed the menu back in its holder. "I'll try the roast beef special."

Hannah self-consciously fidgeted with a belt loop on her jeans, looking almost as unhappy as Tony did. "I'm sorry, we're out of the beef."

"It figures," Tony grumbled to the table.

Maggie nudged Tony's foot in an attempt to jar him out of his preoccupation. "That's what we get for waiting until almost closing time," she said cheerily.

Oblivious, Tony didn't look up. "Just give me a hamburger basket with salad and a cola."

"Is there any custard pie left?" Maggie asked hopefully. Custard pie always helped.

Hannah shook her head. "Only a couple slices of blueberry and one of rhubarb."

Did Tony still love rhubarb pie? Maybe challenging

him for it would get his mind off that meeting. "I'll take the rhubarb."

No response from Tony.

Hannah's rubber-soled sandals squeaking on the gray tile, she walked to the counter and handed the order to Della.

Maggie fidgeted, still no ideas on how to help Tony and Stella popping to mind. "I'll toss you for the rhubarb pie."

"You can have it."

"You don't know what you're missing. And don't expect me to share."

He frowned at her.

At least she'd gotten him to look up. "So what can you cook?"

"Whatever I feel like eating."

"Italian food?"

"Sometimes, although I haven't cooked Italian lately. I have a gas burner, but I cook mostly over a campfire on my building sites."

Finally, he was thinking about something besides his meeting with Stella. "That must be challenging."

"I'm used to it. Locals are eager to share their recipes with me, so I can use ingredients that are readily available."

"So you get to know the local people?"

"Icing on the cake. Talking about food is often a good way to find workers."

"You learn their languages?"

"Some better than others. I hate relying on interpreters any more than I have to."

Asking him about his work was proving to be a good strategy to draw him out. But she couldn't deny she was curious about his life, too. "Do they invite you to their churches?"

"Now and then."

"Do you go?"

"Sometimes." He squinted. "I prefer to worship in His great outdoors. I've found a whole lot fewer judgmental people worship there."

"Still holding on to *that* old grudge?"

"I haven't found any reason to change my mind."

"What about nobody's perfect? Or forgive like you want to be forgiven?" She shifted uncomfortably, recognizing she was having a huge problem with that herself. *Please forgive me.*

Tony lifted an eyebrow as if picking up on her discomfort and trying to make sense of it.

She cleared her throat. "We were talking about your work. You seem to love it."

He shrugged. "Building factories in third-world countries can be challenging, but it has its rewards."

"Do the poverty and poor living conditions get to you?"

"Sure." He studied his spoon. "But many people are intelligent and eager to learn."

"Tell me about them."

"Yeah?"

She nodded encouragement.

The intensity on his face softened. "Well…a couple months ago, I met the neatest little kid in Rio. His name is Paulo. He's ten. He's so proud he can read. The day I met him, he insisted I come home with him to meet his mother, who had taught him. She'd learned from missionaries in the orphanage she grew up in."

"They sound amazing."

"Yeah." He shook his head, his eyes narrowing. "But

they were practically starving. Paulo's father couldn't find enough work to support their ten kids."

"That's so sad. What did you do?"

"I hired him to work for me and helped him move his family to Porto Loges before we started our project."

"That's fantastic, Tony." She liked that he cared about people, in spite of his roaming tendencies. "Is it working out?"

"Better than I ever imagined. Paulo's father is learning to be a good worker, and Paulo and his mother have made it their mission to teach the people of Porto Loges to read. They travel from hut to hut, dragging a half dozen of the kids with them. They need a school."

She wanted that school for Paulo and his mother and the people of Porto Loges. "Is that a possibility?"

He raked his hand through his hair. "I've been trying to interest my backers in helping us fund one. It would only be good business in the long run."

"And?"

He shook his head. "They're balking. But my men and I often chip in for materials and build classrooms in our spare time. So whether my backers jump on board or not, we'll build a school. It will take longer and the school will be smaller with fewer amenities, but we'll make it happen."

"That's wonderful. You're helping people better their lives, just like your nonna does. You're a lot like her."

"Who woulda thought?"

"But won't it be hard to leave Paulo and his family behind when you finish your work there?"

"Can't be helped." He met her gaze. "When the job is done, I move my heavy equipment to the next project. The next country. For the most part, it's a good life."

She frowned, unable to understand how leaving people you cared about could possibly be a good life.

"So why don't you cook?" he asked.

She struggled to follow his sudden change of topic but couldn't help appreciating the shift to something lighter. "With Stella to cook her delicious food for me? You must be joking."

"I'm surprised she hasn't taught you."

"She tried." Maggie made a face. "I was so bad. Even worse than that time you boiled the sauce too long and ruined one of her pans."

"Yeah, she was thrilled," he said sarcastically.

Maggie gave her head a little shake. She couldn't believe she'd brought him right back to Stella being unhappy with him. She desperately needed food to think clearly. "Try not to worry about your nonna, Tony. I'll help you figure out a game plan."

Tony frowned.

"Or maybe you'd rather I stay out of it?"

He shook his head. "I don't have a clue how to fix things with Nonna. But this must set a new record—my needing your help twice in under two hours."

"I'll add it to your bill," she said jokingly.

He held her gaze, no smile in sight. "Will you ever let me pay that?"

Maggie searched his eyes, confused by his serious tone in the face of her joke. She must have missed something. "Pay? How?"

"Maybe need my help for a change?"

"Of course." If he only knew how much she *had* needed him, but how could he? He'd been gone.

Hannah set down their drinks. "Uh, Maggie, is it okay if I invite a friend over to watch a movie tonight?"

"Sure. Janis?"

"No." Hannah drew in a breath and let it out. "Lucas Bradley. He's staying with his grandmother for the summer. She lives by Rainbow Lake. Emma Bradley?"

"Oh, Emma's grandson." Apparently, Hannah had a new friend. A boy. Maggie suppressed a smile. "Sure, you can invite Lucas over. I'll be home all evening."

Hannah threw her a relieved smile. "Thank you." She walked away.

Maggie turned to Tony. "She was so nervous to ask my permission. She's only fifteen." Fifteen had been the most excruciating year of Maggie's life. The year Tony had left. The year she'd lived in Eau Claire with her mom's elderly aunt Bea. The year her parents were killed. The year she'd… She took a quick breath against the jolt of pain.

She'd had nobody left but God. He'd seen her through everything in so many ways. Including giving her Stella, who'd taken her in and treated her like a daughter ever since.

But Tony's fifteenth year hadn't exactly been a lark either. "Don't you remember what being fifteen was like?"

"It was the pits."

"Exactly."

"Maggie McGuire," Della hollered, hustling around the counter and heading for their booth with the energy of a tornado. "Hannah just filled me in on who this handsome stranger is," she boomed across the diner.

"Now the entire town will know I'm back," Tony said under his breath.

Maggie gave him a look. It was probably a good thing they hadn't stopped in at rush hour. "People are interested, that's all."

"Goodness, but you've grown," Della exclaimed, reaching their table.

"Yes, ma'am." Tony climbed to his feet, at least six feet two inches of muscle.

Della's mouth flew open. "And would you look at the manners? Sit back down, honey. When did you get home? Was Stella surprised? What did she say?"

Tony sat, looking up at Della, a confused look on his face.

Maggie decided to help him out. "He just got home about an hour ago. And Stella was thrilled, of course."

Della grinned. "Well, I can imagine. How's she doing?"

Maggie waited for Tony to answer. When he didn't, she jumped in. "She needs lots of rest and therapy."

"No visitors then?"

Maggie thought about how tired Stella looked. "Not for now."

"But if she can do therapy, that has to be good, right?" Della asked with concern.

"Yes, very good," Maggie agreed, not wanting to get bogged down in whether Stella could be motivated to actually do therapy. "How's Rachel?"

"She's getting anxious to have those babies, that's for sure."

Maggie glanced at Tony. "You remember Rachel. Della's daughter?"

"Sure." He frowned as if he didn't have a clue.

He didn't remember Rachel? The pretty blonde classmate he'd taken to homecoming and prom when Maggie's parents insisted Maggie was too young to date?

Della sighed. "Rachel has four boys and is almost due to deliver twin girls."

"Six kids?" He shifted as if uncomfortable with the

thought of Rachel with six kids. Maybe he did remember her after all.

"Her husband travels a lot for his job." Worry laced Della's voice. "Those boys are a real handful, and now—"

The bell on the counter near the cash register pinged. "Nobody here to take my money," Harold Phillips's voice boomed from the counter. "Guess that means we get our pie free tonight."

"Not a chance, Harold," Della called cheerfully. "Tony, you tell your grandma hi for me." Della hustled away.

Hannah set salads in front of them.

"Thanks, Hannah." Maggie picked up her fork.

Tony murmured his thanks and Hannah left.

"Six kids with a father who doesn't have time for them? Why can't parents understand they need to put their kids' needs before their own whims?"

The irony of his words struck her. She knew he was referring to his own father abandoning him. But he had no idea.... A flutter of pain knifing her heart, she speared another mouthful of lettuce.

"You want kids?" Tony asked.

Her salad tasting like sawdust by now, Maggie choked down a bite and concentrated on keeping her voice even. "Someday. Do you?"

"You think my lifestyle is conducive to kids? Or a wife either, for that matter?"

She blew out a breath. "Have you thought about what you'll be missing?"

"My work's important to me." He shrugged. "Anyway, can't miss what you've never had, can you?"

Maggie frowned, the pain in her heart stealing her

breath. She'd held their baby girl only once, and she'd never stopped aching to hold her again.

Would Tony miss his child if he knew he had one? Would he look at every little girl close to her age and wonder what his own daughter was like? Would he long to see her? Wonder if she was happy and loved?

"You okay?" Tony asked.

Crashing back to the present, she met his gaze, considered telling him what his running away and staying lost for five years had cost. After all, the least he could do was share her pain.

Hannah set steaming food in front of them and took their salad plates.

Tony dug in with gusto.

Maggie looked at the best chicken potpie this side of heaven, her appetite in shreds. If not for Hannah's timing, she might very well have lashed out at Tony with the truth.

But he wasn't with her when she'd needed him so desperately. He hadn't even let her know where he was so she could tell him she was pregnant. Or let him know when their baby was born so she could beg him to come home to help her keep their child.

And now?

Dear God, what good could possibly come from telling him he has a daughter ten years after the fact?

Chapter Four

Tony sat at the table in Nonna's ancient kitchen, sounds of a chase scene blaring from Hannah and Lucas's movie in the living room. He stared at the blinking cursor on his laptop. Struggling to keep his mind on his email to his foreman, he keyed in a few more words, deleted them, stared at the cursor again.

Finally, he sat back in his chair and let his gaze drift to the closed door to the small room off the kitchen where Maggie had disappeared when they got home from the diner.

He rubbed the back of his neck. She'd claimed starvation, but when the food came, she'd barely touched it. And gotten really quiet. And now she was hiding. Obviously, something was wrong.

He didn't have to think too hard to figure out a reason. His blowup with Nonna couldn't have been fun to watch. Then she'd tried to cheer him up after his run-in with Nonna, and he'd responded by acting like a jerk. *Nice going, Stefano.*

He stood and strode to the refrigerator. He needed to do something to make it up to her.

* * *

Maggie lay on her stomach on the rug in her little office, doing her best to focus on the computer printouts and financial reports surrounding her. The sounds of speeding cars and gunshots emanated from the living room. But what really messed with her concentration were the occasional small sounds Tony made in the kitchen.

Well, the fact that he was in the kitchen at all.

She understood why Stella wanted him to stay in his childhood home, but that didn't mean his being here wasn't causing havoc with Maggie's nerves. She blew out a breath. Having him home was…difficult.

Doing her best to focus on her notes, she squinted in the dim glow cast by the beautiful, old crystal ceiling light. Trimming this, tucking that from her budget, she'd eked out the few thousand dollars she needed for the downstairs bathroom. But as hard as she looked, she just couldn't afford to cut anything else to pay for additional repairs the house needed.

She'd have to go deeper in debt. But financial risk was a small price to pay compared to risking Stella's will to recover. Ignoring the tension cramping her shoulders, she flipped the page of her yellow notepad and continued outlining a plan to present to a loan officer to prove she qualified for another loan.

A rap on the door made her drop her pencil.

"How long are you planning to hide?" Tony's low voice rumbled.

His voice sent an uneasy tingle along her nerves. Frowning, she shook her head. "I'm working, and I don't want to be interrupted."

"Can I help?"

Just what she needed. "Thanks, but I don't think so."

A pause.

"Look, Maggie…I'm sorry I was such a jerk at the diner."

"You weren't a jerk."

"Yes, I was. What happened? I could always count on the truth from you."

Apparently, things had changed. She drew in a deep breath. "All right. You were *kind* of a jerk. Apology accepted. Now, I really need to get back to work."

"Come on, Blossom. I'm trying to make it up to you. And I thought maybe we could talk about that game plan you said you'd help me with. Will you let me in?"

"Can't. Sorry."

"Come on, Maggie. Apologizing through a door is the pits."

The very last thing she needed was his invading her office. If not wanting to see him wasn't enough, her office was a mess. The desk, the floor…papers were spread all over. And she didn't want him figuring out what she was up to either. He'd only give her more grief about putting money into Stella's house. "Sorry."

"I'm coming in at the count of three."

Touching the towel turban wrapping her head, she looked down at her Green Bay Packers shirt and lounging pants. No. Absolutely not. "Don't you dare."

"One."

If only the door had a working lock. She dropped the notepad. Call it vanity, but she didn't want him seeing her like this. "I'm not decent."

"Then get decent."

"Tony, I'm warning you…" She began unclasping the towel on her head. Not good. Her hair had mostly dried by now and would be squiggled in all directions. She hated that.

"Two."

She glanced around the room. No place to hide and no way to escape except through the window.

"Three. You decent yet?"

With a sigh, she reclasped the towel. Avoiding the reports and papers stacked in untidy piles, she scrambled to sit up, her legs tucked under her. "All right. Come in if you must."

The door opened wide. He filled the doorway like a stalwart oak—tall and sturdy and strong. But the restless tension in his muscles was incompatible with any oak she'd ever seen. His thick black hair was tousled, his brawny chest and biceps strained the fabric of his black T-shirt, his jeans hugged narrow hips and muscular thighs. His presence filled the room.

She drew a breath. *Dear God, please help me get rid of him without letting him see how frazzled he makes me feel.*

Balancing a tray with two glasses of soda on it, he gave her an apologetic little grin. "My peace offering."

"Thank you, I think," she stammered. "But like I said, I'm working, so my heart is occupied." Heart? Had she said heart? "Head. My head is occupied."

He gave her a little frown and scanned the room. "It looks like you had an explosion in here."

"Lots of work." She watched him zero in on the colorful paper and magazine cutouts on her desk.

"Work?"

"I'm making posters for the dairy breakfast. It's the big church benefit for the summer."

"Ah, I guess that explains why you're working on the floor. But what are you working on?"

"Stuff."

"None of my business?" An amused smirk danced

around his full lips. His smirk breaking into a grin, he balanced the tray in one hand, bent to pick up a stack of papers and smoothly lowered himself to the floor without spilling a drop of soda.

Power, grace and efficiency all wrapped in a body of steel. Too bad his roots were as shallow as a poplar's. From the letters and emails he began sending Stella five years ago, Maggie knew he hadn't stayed in one place very long.

She tore her gaze from his impressive biceps to look at the tray he'd set beside her. He'd actually found a bud vase and cut one of the yellow antique roses climbing the front porch. His thoughtful gestures had always melted her heart. Tears stinging her eyes, she did her best to hide her feelings by bending to smell the musky scent of the old-fashioned rose. "I see you still have an artist's eye."

"Thank you. I recognize beauty when I see it." Handing her a glass of soda, a smile spread across his face.

She caught her lips returning his smile and whipped them into line. She took a sip of soda, carbonation tickling her nose and adding to her discomfort. "Thank you for the soda, but I really need to work."

"You're dismissing me?"

"Your insight amazes me."

Reaching for a stack of papers beside her, his hand brushed her arm.

Her stomach did a flip. A wave of panic threatened. How was she going to get him out of there?

Hannah popped her head in the door. "I'm making popcorn for Lucas and me. You guys want some?"

"Thanks," Tony answered. "I never turn down popcorn."

"Okay." Hannah looked at Maggie. "How many minutes should I set the microwave for?"

"Push the popcorn button on the microwave. It does all the timing for you."

"Thanks." Hannah bustled away.

A brief interruption but it gave Maggie a chance to get her bearings. What had her in such a tizzy anyway? It wasn't like she'd never been alone with a man before.

Of course, this wasn't just any man, she reminded herself. This was Tony. Her first love. The boy who'd left her behind without caring about her tender heart. The man who still loved roaming the world like a gypsy.

She needed to pull herself together so she could figure out a way to get him out of her office. Maybe discussing what he could do about his nonna would give him something to mull over so he'd leave. "About Stella, Tony…"

"Yeah…" He looked intently into her eyes.

Her mouth suddenly going dry, she swallowed and hung on to her bearings. "You do know you have to keep your dad out of any conversation with her, don't you?"

"Fine by me. She's the one who keeps bringing him up."

"You need to change the subject."

"I tried," he said emphatically. "You were there."

"Well, in the future, change to something the two of you agree on."

"Like what?"

"Good question." She sighed. "Not moving from the house."

He narrowed his gaze. "You already made your point on that."

"Not Noah's Crossing. Or doctors. Or South America." Slowly, a plan began to unfold in her mind. "Maybe it would help if she could see you're working toward her coming home where she wants to be."

"Are you talking about her house again?"

She nodded. "What about the ramp? I'm sure you could build one in a matter of hours. We could take a picture of it to show her."

Scowling, he shook his head. "Her house is just plain inadequate for her. Period."

She gave him an "oh, please" look. "The ramp would show her you care what *she* wants."

He rubbed the back of his neck. "Come on, Maggie, give me a plan I can get behind."

She threw up her hands. "You traveled all the way from Brazil to make peace with your nonna. To make that happen, did it ever occur to you that at least one of you is going to have to bend?"

He leveled his gaze on her. "Then it will have to be me."

"Absolutely."

"Oh, boy." He rammed his fingers through his hair. "We never agreed on anything…but food."

A lightbulb idea. "There you go. Stella loves Della's sticky buns. Start by taking her some of those. A small plan, but one you can expand on."

He studied the rug for several seconds, then raised his gaze to meet hers. "I guess it's worth a try. Thanks, Blossom. I could always count on you."

"You're the one who thought about food." Now he'd leave so she could get back to her plan. She glanced around for her yellow notepad.

"Will you go with me to see her tomorrow?" Tony asked.

"Do you promise to behave?"

"Cross my heart." He soberly drew an *x* across his chest with his finger.

Her gaze got stuck first on his fingers, then on his broad chest. She scrambled to remember Stella's schedule. "Stella's physical therapy is at nine. She'll need rest afterward. How about meeting me at the rehab center about eleven?"

"Eleven it is. I appreciate it, Maggie."

"I'll add it to your bill." Done. Over. Out.

"Right." He dropped his gaze to the stack of papers he'd balanced on his knees. "'Scapes by Design.' Looks like a landscaping business. Yours?"

"Yes. You can put those down." She pointed to indicate where he should put the reports, her gaze scanning the area for the yellow pad with her notes for getting a loan.

He turned and put down the stack of papers, pausing to look at a report in another stack. "*And* you own a plant retail outlet? 'Magnolia's Blossoms'?" He grinned. "Nice name. Two businesses must keep you busy. No wonder you're working tonight."

She frowned. He'd *never* been this chatty. "And I have more work to do," she said pointedly.

He ignored her comment. "Nonna wrote that you sold your parents' hardware store after they died. But how did you pull off two businesses?"

"Weren't you about to leave so I can get back to work?"

"I'm interested in what you've been up to since I went away. Something you don't want me to know about?"

"Not at all." Not about her businesses anyway. She was proud of what she'd accomplished. She sighed. It seemed he was set on hanging out and no amount of plan solving was going to budge him.

"So you sold the hardware store and…"

"You are every bit as stubborn as Stella can be when she wants me to open up." She tossed him an irritated glance.

"Then talk to me, Blossom. Do you have any idea how far it is from Brazil to Wisconsin? Yet, here I am."

"You're trying to make me feel guilty?"

"Just reminding you of your manners. After all, technically, I *am* your guest."

She rolled her eyes.

"So you sold the hardware store and…" he repeated, giving her a look that said he didn't plan to budge anytime soon.

She guessed she might just as well talk. "I hated selling the store, but I didn't know much about hardware and absolutely nothing about running a business."

"Understandable. You were just a kid."

After all she'd been through at that point, "just a kid" hardly described her. "Stella and her lawyer thought I should put the money from the store away for college. But I decided to pay off the mortgage on the farm instead, then I borrowed against the farm for tuition when I needed it. And I worked for a landscaper in the summers."

"Smart. Did you graduate in landscape architecture?"

She nodded. "Then I worked for a landscaping company in Madison for a year to gain experience and pay off a chunk of my college debts."

"You must have had a lot of options. Why in the world did you come back to Noah's Crossing?"

His disparaging tone set her teeth on edge. She shot him a narrow look.

He raised his eyebrow. "What I mean is, opening a business is risky. You're obviously making a success of not one but two. What made you think you could pull it off *here?*"

He seemed sincere enough. "I had the farm. Noah's Crossing was growing *and* didn't have a landscaping company. It's the best decision I ever made. I love Noah's Crossing."

"Ambitious woman." He ignored her last comment. No surprise there.

"Those new houses on Doc Tilbert's place. Did you do their landscaping?"

"Most of them. I didn't like seeing his farm developed, even if it did help me whittle down the loan I'd taken against the farm for start-up capital. So when I needed a better source for landscaping plants last summer, I built the greenhouse and started my own retail plant outlet." She took a sip of soda and set the glass on the tray.

He picked up the yellow notepad and studied it.

The pad with her notes on it? Where had it been?

"This looks like a plan to get a loan."

She didn't need another argument about Stella's house. She reached for the tablet.

He gave it to her. "I suppose you've figured out you can't swing a loan."

"My, aren't I lucky I won't be applying to you to get one?" she asked sarcastically.

"You have significant assets to protect. You can't afford to flirt with being overextended. What do you need another loan for anyway?"

"None of your business."

"You're trying to find money to sink into this place?"

"You don't need to worry about it, Tony. I'm working on a plan."

He gave a grunt of obvious disapproval.

She ignored it. "I can make Stella's ten acres pay off by hiring more employees to plant gardens and tend the flowers—"

"A catch-22." He set his empty glass on the tray. "Will you have cash flow to meet payroll for more employees until the land starts paying off?"

He'd zeroed right in on the problem. Obviously, he had a good head for business.

He tapped the paper with his index finger. "So far, you're doing a great job making debt work for you. I know if I hadn't gone into debt, I wouldn't have been able to buy my first piece of heavy equipment. But you're already carrying a heavy load. You could risk your whole operation going under."

Unfortunately, her head told her he was right. But her heart, well, her heart couldn't afford to listen. Not with Stella counting on coming back to her home. "I'll find a way to make it work."

His rugged features softened. "You still never give up, do you, Blossom?"

The warmth in his tone stirred memories of the deep connection they'd shared. Of secrets revealed, pacts forged, calamities overcome. He'd understood her, accepted her, encouraged her when she'd messed up.

And even with all the tension hanging between them now, she couldn't deny she missed him even more than she'd realized.

Tony thumped his pillow with his fist and did his best to cling to his dream. In it, he and Maggie were all grown up. They were in her tree house again. And they were just about to kiss.

He swiped his hand across his face to discourage the annoyance. Dream vanishing, he realized somebody was dripping water on him. Wide-awake now, he sat upright to confront the prankster.

A flash of lightning lit up the windows lining three walls in the upstairs three-season porch. Thunder crashed. The dull plop of dripping water droned around him. He'd heard that sound too many nights in the rain forest not to recognize it. The roof was leaking. Big-time.

It had been too dark to check the roof when he'd given the place a once-over after leaving Maggie in her office. He hauled himself out of the small, old-fashioned bed, pulled on his jeans and flipped on the light switch by the door.

A dim glow from the ancient ceiling fixture did little to chase away the deep shadows. But he could make out water running along a crack in the ceiling and un-loading directly over his bed. Judging from the musty smell, the sagging roof and the stained plaster in many of the rooms, the leaks weren't limited to the flat roof covering this room.

Turning on his heel, he walked barefoot into the hall and switched on the light. If he could find a flashlight, the rain would make it easy to inspect the attic to see how bad the leaking problem was.

One more thing to add to the list of reasons Maggie should not be thinking about spending money on this place. Somehow, he had to make her listen.

She'd been wired as tight as a fiddle string in her office tonight. But being with her had triggered memories of how close they'd once been. So close, they'd often finished each other's sentences.

Where would they be if he'd stayed? Married? Maybe with several kids? Would he feel trapped? Would she?

Striding down the hall past her closed door, he wondered if she was dreaming about him. He grunted. Fat chance. Her dreams probably centered around profit-and-loss statements and this old house. He sprinted down the stairs, switched on lights to illuminate the way and assaulted the kitchen cabinets in search of a flashlight.

Thunder rumbled low and ominous. Lights flickered. The electricity had better hold, at least until he found a flashlight.

"Shh. You'll wake Hannah." Maggie's soft voice, heavy with sleep, drifted to him. "What are you doing?"

He drew back from the cupboard and peered at her. Her copper curls stood on end, jutting in all directions in little corkscrews. She sure looked cute. "Sorry, I didn't mean to wake you, Blossom. Do you know where I can find a flashlight?"

As if in a fog, she padded barefoot to the back door, took a flashlight from the shelf above the coatrack and brought it to him. "Why do you need a flashlight?"

He took the light. "I need to check out the attic for leaks. The roof on the three-season porch is a sieve."

She frowned. "Sorry about that. But do you have to check the attic in the middle of the night?"

"The rain will make it easy to see where the leaks are." Even better idea, *she* could see the leaking roof firsthand. He eyed her bare feet, remembering how freaked out she'd been the time a June bug attached itself to her pinkie toe. "Why don't you come along? But you might want to put on some shoes first."

"You aren't wearing shoes."

"You aren't worried you'll step on a bug or something?"

She dismissed his warning with the wave of her hand. "I'm not afraid of bugs anymore."

Hmm. "What about mice and rats? Have you outgrown your fear of those, too?"

She turned to give him a blistering look. "There aren't any rats in Stella's house."

"You sure?"

She pursed her mouth as it apparently dawned on her he might be teasing.

It occurred to him that he'd never seen more delectable lips.

She frowned. "Let's go."

He forced his mind back to the issue at hand. The rain. Showing her the leaks in the attic. The rats. "All I need is a weapon."

"What for?"

"For the rats."

"Tony—" She gave him a look that told him she wasn't going to take the bait again.

He peered at her with exaggerated gravity. "Rats are one thing I've learned to expect on building sites, and I'm seldom disappointed. Even though I'm not one to brag about my exploits, I've single-handedly managed to exterminate large numbers of them."

She shivered. "This is one of the reasons you enjoy exploring faraway places so much?"

He laughed. "Believe me, no place is nearly as threatening as the stagnation of good old Noah's Crossing."

She gave him a look and closed her eyes as if to shut out what she didn't want to hear.

Teasing her was fun, but he probably shouldn't have

made that crack about Noah's Crossing. He strode over and opened the closet where Nonna kept cleaning tools when he was a boy. Apparently, she still did. He grabbed a broom and raised it over his head. "My weapon."

She laughed a hearty, mellow sound that touched a responsive chord deep within him. "Well, Blossom, if you're up to taking on the dangers that lurk in Nonna's attic, follow me."

Pumping the broom like a baton, he marched up the steps, Maggie padding softly behind him. He led the way down the hall, through the door to the attic stairs and followed the beam of his flashlight up the narrow staircase into the hot, humid attic.

The distinct odor of rotting wood rode the air before he heard the drone of dripping water. Stepping onto the planked floor, he swept the flashlight beam across pans and cans of every conceivable size and shape dutifully collecting water streaming from the ceiling. "What is all this?"

"Containers to catch the water. We empty them and put them back for the next rain."

He stared at her. "That's how you handle the leaky roof? Just empty the cans to catch more rain?"

"Stella is one to make do. There's a big dry area on the other side." She pointed. "We keep anything of value there."

"Great plan," he grumbled. Sweeping his light to the ceiling, it spread over large areas of soaked, blackened wood. It was even worse than he'd expected. And a perfect picture for Maggie. "Would you look at that. The rafters are rotting. See?"

He ran the light along a rafter, giving her time to see the destruction. Then he focused the beam on the unplanked area of the floor. "The batts of insulation are compacted and discolored, too. No doubt, the subfloor under them is rotted and the plaster throughout the house is soaked, which explains the stains I saw. Add that to corroded plumbing and electric wires so crisp with age they're a fire waiting to happen, and you've got a very big problem."

"You're exaggerating."

Everywhere he ran the flashlight beam, he spotted more damage. "I don't need to exaggerate. You wouldn't believe what I found when I did a survey of the old place after I left your office. Maggie, this house is about to fall down around your ears."

"Don't be silly." She sounded as if she was talking through clenched teeth.

"The entire top of the house needs to be ripped off and built new." He turned to her, expecting her to concede that he was right about the house. And if she needed comforting, he was definitely up to the task.

But there she stood, her spine as stiff as a pole, her chin as lofty as the highest beam and her head totally in the clouds. "If all that has to be done, it has to be done."

He stared in disbelief. "It would cost a fortune."

"Then I'll find a way to get it."

She wasn't dense. Or *that* stubborn. He narrowed his eyes, ready to hammer home his point.

She put up her hand as if to stop him. "Your nonna is my family. After my parents died in the car accident, she took me in. Just like that. She's loved me like a daughter. Given me roots. I don't know what I'd have done without her. And I don't know what I'd do without her now." Her brown eyes sparkled with tears.

Please…not tears. Her tears had always done weird things to him. Still did. He'd never had a clue how to deal with them. Still didn't. He stepped closer and put his arm around her shoulders.

She leaned into him. "Tony, she gave me everything when I needed her. Now she needs me. And I will never let that wonderful woman down."

Her fierce loyalty had always taken his breath away. The loyalty she'd once given him. "Nonna's lucky to have you, Maggie."

"I'm the lucky one. She has to get better. She has to."

"You think if she can come back to her house, it will help her get well. But you can't change the facts about this place."

Maggie raised her chin a notch, a sure sign she'd made up her mind. "With God's help, I will do whatever I have to."

She would, too. And God pity the man who stood in her way.

Chapter Five

Maggie drove west, listening to a client on her speakerphone. The scent of earth and growing plants rode the hot breeze blowing through the window. Puffy white clouds floated in the late-afternoon sky. Variegated greens of June danced across hills and fields.

But Maggie's frame of mind was anything but carefree. Although this morning's meeting between Stella and Tony hadn't featured fireworks, Stella was tired and irritable and she'd refused her nine o'clock physical-therapy session. Tony's offering of sticky buns had been only a marginal hit. He'd teamed up with Maggie to try to lift Stella's spirits, but they hadn't succeeded.

Maggie dragged her attention back to her client's nervous chatter on the speaker. It was a beautiful Saturday, but just another workday in the busy landscaping season. "Please let me do the worrying, Mrs. Dobbs. It's one of the things you're paying me for. I just called to tell you to expect my crew Monday at 6:00 a.m. sharp." She ended the call.

She pushed her speed-dial and squinted into the sun, noticing a big puff of blackish smoke billowing ahead. Somebody must be burning garbage. Lots of it.

"Physical Therapy. This is Jim."

"Hi, Jim. How did it go with Stella this afternoon?"

"I was about to call you. She refused physical therapy again. Her occupational therapist coaxed her to try, but Stella had trouble concentrating. And I just checked. She's sacked out for the night. She didn't have the best day."

Tension grabbed between Maggie's shoulder blades. Did Stella's day have anything to do with last night's argument with Tony? Had they argued today after she'd left them? "She needs to do her therapy to get well. What can I do?"

"Keep on doing what you're doing. Stop in for short visits. Keep bringing flowers that remind her of her garden and her home. Whatever you think might motivate her. It's important we don't let her give up."

Maggie nodded as if he could see her. Jim had been her rock ever since Stella's accident.

"Are you headed home, Maggie?"

"Yes."

"Want to meet at the diner for a quick bite?"

"Not tonight. I'm beat. I'm going to settle for a sandwich and go to bed early."

"How about tomorrow night? We could drive to Dun Harbor and take in a movie. Might be just what the doctor ordered. Want to go?"

"Tomorrow probably won't work. Stella's grandson is home."

"Oh? Tony's back? How long is he staying?"

"He's staying only a week."

A pause stretched between them. "Well, maybe we can take in that movie next weekend then?"

Jim was such a nice guy, and she knew he liked her and wanted to start a relationship. Trouble was, she didn't know how she felt about that. And she certainly wasn't prepared to think about it at the moment. "We'll see."

"Fair enough."

She felt bad at the disappointment in his voice.

"Try not to worry about Stella," he said. "Let's hope she does better tomorrow."

Maggie clicked off, worry and weariness clouding her mind and tugging at her limbs. She'd traipsed around a client's garden all afternoon. She was sweaty, her shoes were muddy, her gray slacks were rumpled and her blouse had a smudge. She'd fallen a long way from the polished professional image she strove to project, which didn't seem important compared to Stella's welfare.

The black billow of smoke still hung in the sky like a dark premonition. It seemed awfully close to Stella's place. Tony's comment on the electrical wiring being a fire waiting to happen hovered in her mind.

She could smell it now. A foul odor, but without the sweet tinge of burning garbage. It couldn't be the house, could it? Tony wouldn't—no. Maybe he was burning the old sheds. The close proximity of two towering hickories to the buildings flitted into her mind. Surely, he'd realize he couldn't burn the sheds where they stood.

Taking the big curve, Maggie could see the smoke rose from behind the house, farther away than the sheds. She breathed a sigh of relief.

She turned into the driveway and pulled alongside Tony's motorcycle. She shut off the engine, jumped out and strode around the house. The boards for the ramp were gone. But they were new boards. Why would he burn those?

She turned to look for the trail of smoke. It drifted up just beyond the woods.

The wildflower meadow? Her mind shot into overload. The beautiful prairie plants that had taken years to establish were thriving gloriously. Interrupting them now would probably kill them.

She took off at a jog, winding her way through the trees. He wouldn't realize how much time and effort ridding the meadow of weed competitors had taken. But surely, he'd recognize wildflowers when he saw them.

She reached the clearing, warm and a little out of breath. Twenty feet away, thick black smoke billowed from a huge mound of smoldering rubble, a languid flame licking the edges. The burning heap lay smack-dab in the middle of an explosion of blue false indigo.

How could he destroy a field of living plants? Especially plants as beautiful as these? When she got her hands on him…

A shape took form, striding from behind the blanket of smoke. Tony. In jeans and work boots, his bronze chest streaked with dirt and soot. "Hi, Blossom. Didn't hear you drive in."

Sweaty, reeking of smoke, he looked like a pillaging warrior. And he loomed over her, his mere presence a force to be reckoned with.

She'd reckon with him, all right. Just as soon as she caught her breath. "How could you? How *could* you?"

Hanging his big hands on his slim hips, he looked around blankly. "How could I what?"

"What do you think you're doing?"

"Burning my past. You should try it sometime."

She shifted her gaze to the fire, homed in on gold nuggets glinting in the sun on the top of the smoldering heap. Buttons of a navy blue uniform trimmed with red-

and-white braid. "You're burning your band uniform?" she sputtered in disbelief.

"Several sizes." He bent and grasped the contents of one of the boxes at his feet. "Nonna must have thought I'd have some use for my father's old sheet music for violin. I don't." He threw the stack, sheet music fanning out and floating down into the fire, the edges crinkling and turning brown.

Maggie wanted to tell him he might someday wish he'd kept something so important to his father. Instead, she dragged an agitated breath of hot, smoky air, the sight of her beautiful indigos crumpling in the heat re-igniting her anger. She pointed an accusing finger at the pile. "Do you have any idea what you're doing?"

Eyeing her warily, he cocked one of those irritating eyebrows. "What has you so steamed?"

"Look around you. What do you see?"

He half turned, squinting at his handiwork. "A fire… burning junk."

"What else?" She spotted a rake near the pile and strode to pick it up. Raking the edges of the fire to prevent it from spreading, she waited for him to notice the variety of tall grasses waving in the breeze, the brilliant yellow lanceleaf coreopsis covering the southern slope, the white sea of delicate shooting stars near the indigos.

"What are you doing?" he demanded.

"Trying to contain the fire."

"Why?"

She waved a hand to encompass the beauty around him. "What do you see?" she repeated.

"I see an open field."

"No, Tony, that's not what you see." Her voice had taken on a lethal quiet she didn't recognize.

He scowled.

She drew in another deep breath of scorching air in an attempt to calm herself. It didn't work. "You are looking at a wildflower meadow that has taken Stella and me years to establish."

He scanned the meadow and the burning heap of rubble, then settled his comprehending gaze on her face. "Whoops." He grabbed the rake from her and beat out flames licking the edges of the fire. "It looked like an open field to me."

"Didn't the flowers give you a clue this field might be somewhat different than just any field?"

Raking hard, he prevented the fire from expanding to consume any more of the flowers. "We have a hard time clearing land in the rain forest. Flowers and plants grow everywhere, big ones, exotic ones—all wild. I had no idea these were valuable to anyone. Honest."

He swiped his free hand across his brow, leaving a streak of soot in its wake, and peered at her with what might be construed as guilt. "I'll make it up to you."

She shook her head, raising her chin in as haughty a pose as she could muster. "Did you burn the boards, too? The ones for the ramp?"

"Why would I burn perfectly good boards? Although some of them are warped because of last night's rain. I stored them in the shed that's not falling down." He drew in a deep breath. "*Can* I do anything to make it up to you for burning your flowers?"

She looked him straight in those black eyes. "You can help me get your nonna's house ready for her to come home."

"You know I can't do that in good conscience. But I *will* help you look for a one-story house for the two of you to move into."

She harrumphed. She hadn't even bothered to get her

hopes up. She spotted part of a rickety trellis that Stella had stored in one of the sheds, probably for sentimental reasons. She pointed. "You're burning Stella's trellis?"

"She never used it," he said glumly.

"How do you know? She's kept it forever. Maybe Salvatore made it for her."

"I made it in my eighth-grade manual arts class for her roses. She loved it so much, she had me plant beans to grow on it." He glared at Maggie, obviously wanting to make sure she got his point.

"I'm sorry," she murmured.

"Don't be. It's just a rickety old trellis, which is why I'm burning it."

She swallowed, knowing it had meant a lot more to him than he'd admit. "But you have to consider how long she's saved it."

The fire popped. She stared at shattered glass of a picture frame. A frame holding a portrait of his father. Horrified, she reached to retrieve it, but heat made her take her hand away. She watched the edges of the picture curl and catch fire.

What was wrong with him? He seemed bent on destroying his past as though it was some kind of dark, despicable thing. "Do you really think the bad memories will go away if you burn things that remind you of them?"

His jaw clenched. "I can always hope."

The desolation in his voice doused her anger like a cold rain. She stared at him. His eyes were serious. Deadly serious. He was in pain, and he honestly didn't know what to do about it. "Tony..." She wanted to put her arms around him to comfort him. Bad idea.

Help me find a way to help him, God. She searched for words that made sense. "You know, your past, good and bad, will always be with you. It's what makes you who you are."

He gave her a wary look. "Don't wax philosophical on me, Blossom."

She caught herself up short. He'd always run from emotional issues like he'd run from Noah's Crossing. But why wouldn't he if all they brought him was pain? A little scheme began hatching in her mind.

He narrowed his eyes. "I can almost see the wheels spinning in your brain."

"Where's Stella's trunk?"

"The one in the attic?"

She was afraid to ask, but she had to know. "Did you burn it?"

He scowled. "Give me some credit. I'm not burning Nonna's things."

Deciding against reminding him that he'd burned his nonna's trellis, she drew in a deep breath. Maybe, just maybe, some of the things in that trunk would reconnect Tony with good memories of his past, his home. "I'll show you what's in that trunk."

"All I saw in there were old financial journals and some ancient clothes and scrapbooks and letters. Nothing valuable."

She shook her head. He had no clue. "Stella keeps her very best treasures in that trunk. Treasures you need to see."

Tony followed Maggie up the narrow attic stairs, the temperature climbing with each step. He'd tried to talk her out of coming up here. But she wouldn't listen to his argument that he needed to tend the fire, not when the fire was almost out and was contained by the charred grass around it.

Seemed she was bent on rifling through that old trunk before another moment passed.

Her lack of logic baffled him. She'd returned to this little town when she had enough smarts and education to make a success of her life anywhere in the world. She clung to her belief that the dilapidated old house was the only thing that would save Nonna. And she seemed incapable of understanding why the soaring temperature in the attic just might be a deterrent to spending time up here.

Maybe her blood sugar was low. "Hey, Blossom, how about eating supper before we go through that trunk? I'll demonstrate my talents in the kitchen."

"It'll be too dark if we eat first. Even with the gable windows, the light is dim enough now." She reached the top step and strode across the planks, careful to avoid the pots and cans strategically placed to catch the rain from leaks in the roof.

He followed, admiring her reflection in the full-length mirror standing near the battered trunk in the dry area of the attic. She sure did look determined. She'd always gotten determined over things. A trait that had kept life interesting growing up.

She turned to him. "We can eat first, if you want to move the trunk downstairs for later."

He glanced at the huge box, then sized up the narrow stairs. "It's too wide. Somebody must have built that thing up here. But I'm starved. And I could be whipping up my world-class marinara sauce instead of lingering in this sweltering attic."

She gave him a condescending look. "Try to cope, Tony. Hannah will be home soon and she'll eat with us. Anyway, I doubt you'll collapse from hunger if we eat in an hour. An hour *if* you give your undivided attention to these treasures."

"You drive a hard bargain."

"It's the least you can do. I'm sure I needn't remind you how many years of work and careful tending you reduced to ashes?"

"No, you don't need to remind me."

"I didn't think so."

She was a stubborn woman when she set her mind to something. He might as well try to ignore the sweltering heat and his rumbling stomach and settle in for the duration. He leaned against a gable beam, one of the few that wasn't succumbing to water damage. Yet.

She bent over the ancient trunk and moved the wire hangers he'd taken his old clothes from. His band uniforms in graduated sizes, likewise his baseball uniforms. Thankfully, he was better at baseball than he'd been at football, but not by much.

"I see you thought the hangers were worth saving." Maggie's soft voice held a chuckle.

"Why not? They can be put to some use."

She lifted the hinged lid, dropped to her knees and rummaged inside the trunk. She unfolded a small blue dress and held it aloft. She smoothed its folds almost reverently, a dreamy look in her eyes. "Stella wore this gown to her first opera in Italy when she was eleven. Her father surprised her with a yellow rose, and she saw Puccini's *Tosca*. She says it was the most beautiful memory of her life until she met Salvatore."

Tony could swear Maggie had tears in her eyes. She teared up almost as much as she blushed. He eyed the dress. It looked limp and old and wrinkled. Not at all like the young, vibrant woman holding it up for him to admire. Her slacks and blouse were rumpled and a little smudged, but she had to work hard physically to stay so trim. That and not eat, like now. "Very nice."

Looking pleased, she set aside the dress and blew her hair off her forehead. She reached into the trunk again and came up with one of the old scrapbooks Nonna had always wanted him to look at growing up. It appeared avoidance had come to an end.

Head bent, Maggie smiled as she carefully turned pages.

She wasn't getting teary again, was she?

"These are amazing," she said. Beaming like sunshine, she stood up and leaned to show him the book. Seemed she was actually enjoying taking the time to show him his history.

Would it kill him to act a little interested? He could handle it…for Maggie. His gaze flitted over a couple pages of baby pictures with a plane ticket attached to each one. He didn't get it. "What are these?"

Maggie smiled up at him. "They're pictures Stella and Salvatore snapped of you and the tickets for the flights they took to visit you. Look at how adorable you were."

Breathing in Maggie's subtle scent, his hand glazed her arm as he reached around her to turn a ticket so he could see its destination. Vienna.

"I'd say you were a much-loved grandson to warrant your grandparents flying around the world to see you, wouldn't you?"

Did she sound a little breathless, or was it just his imagination? "Pretty impressive," he admitted.

"You should take these albums with you when you go to see her. She'd love it."

Yeah, if he ever had an attack of wanting to delve into the past with Nonna. "Maybe," he said evasively.

Leaving the book in his hands, she returned to the trunk and came back with a haphazard frame made from Popsicle sticks enclosing a picture of him at around four. "Your nonna saved this, too," Maggie said.

A warm memory of his mother sifted through his mind. "My mother helped me make that," he said quietly.

Maggie gave him the sweetest smile he'd ever seen. "A wonderful memory."

"Yeah." A memory he enjoyed remembering. He handed her the album he held.

She took it and the framed picture back to the trunk, this time bringing another album. She turned the page, then peered at him, apparently studying his features. Damp tendrils of copper hair clung to her temples and neck, and a fine sheen of perspiration shone from the smattering of freckles sprinkled across her turned-up nose.

He wanted very much to touch each one of those freckles.

She pointed to an old photo. "This must have been taken when your great-grandfather was about your age. Your resemblance to him is remarkable."

"You'd think we were related," he said dryly. But having her full attention on him was feeling better and better. Besides, he liked her comment that he looked like his great-grandfather. That idea was a whole lot more palatable than looking like his dad as Nonna claimed.

"Look, Tony…a picture of Salvatore in his army uniform." Holding the scrapbook for him to see, she pointed to a picture.

He peered at it, his gaze wandering to the one beside it of an impressive-looking horse named Dolly, if he remembered correctly. Then his gaze moved to a photo of his father, mother and him at about three. Dressed to the nines and standing in front of Nonna's house, his statuesque mother smiled at his father, who was wearing a tux and beaming up at the scrubbed and polished boy perched on his shoulder.

A distant memory floated through his mind. The memory of riding on his father's shoulders, his mother laughing and warning him to duck so he wouldn't hit his head on the door frame.

His throat tightened until he couldn't breathe. He needed to get out of here. "It's getting too dark to see these."

Maggie looked up at him. "Do you remember this?"

He dragged in a gulp of scorching air.

"Oh, Tony. You lost so much when your mother died, but it's good to remember there were happy times," she said, her voice hushed and gentle.

He shook his head. "If it's so good to remember, why does it make me want to slam my fist into something—preferably my father's face?"

"Maybe you blame him for taking away those happy times."

"Why wouldn't I? He was a selfish man whose main concern when my mother died was getting on with his violin tour. Not to mention the times he promised to come back and take me with him and never even visited."

"He could have planned to—"

"Don't defend him, Maggie." He gave her a deadly look. "Not to me."

She pressed her fingers to her lips as if to silence them.

"Nothing can change the truth I've always known in here." He thumped his chest over his heart.

"What truth?"

Did he really want to tell her his deepest thoughts?

"What truth, Tony?" she asked again.

He blew out a breath. If he couldn't tell Maggie, who could he tell? "He didn't love me."

"What?" Maggie stared at him. "Of course he loved you. You can see it in his face in the picture. His love for you didn't just disappear when your mom died."

"What happened to it, then?" He grasped the album and pointed to the picture. "How could he look at me like that and then turn his back on me?"

Maggie bit her lip, her eyes clouding. "I don't know, Tony. How did you do it?"

He stared at her. Had she said what he thought she had?

Pressing her fingers to her lips, she shook her head.

But he'd heard her. He shut his eyes, turning her accusation over in his mind. Was she right? Had he deserted Maggie just like his father had deserted him?

Chapter Six

Maggie's heart beat so hard she could scarcely breathe. She hadn't meant to blurt her feelings out loud. But there they were. And the shock on Tony's face did nothing to make her feel better.

"I need to get that sauce on the stove if we're going to eat tonight," he said brusquely.

He wanted to get out of Dodge ASAP. Nothing new there. But she couldn't let him go. Not with her accusation hanging between them. "Tony, I think we need to talk about this. Please stay."

He closed his eyes again as if he wanted to shut himself away. "I should never have made love to you that day. I'd promised your dad I'd take care of you."

"You always took care of me."

Shaking his head, he met her gaze. "You were too young."

"You were only two years older than me. We could have talked about it, couldn't we?"

He gave her a puzzled look. "Talked about it?"

"If you'd stayed."

"I figured if I didn't leave that night, I would be stuck

in Noah's Crossing for a very long time. Maybe in jail if the sheriff had his way."

Stuck in Noah's Crossing…with her. She did her best to push away the hurt. "You could have written."

"I let Nonna know I was okay. I figured she'd tell you or your parents."

She shook her head, wanting to stamp her foot in frustration. "You didn't tell her where you were, and it took you five years to write again. A lot can happen in five years, Tony." She dragged in a shaky breath. "A lot can happen in a year."

"I'm sorry I didn't know about your parents' car accident. I'm sure you had a rough time losing them so suddenly." He ran his hand over her face. "I don't want to make excuses, Maggie, but I just couldn't let Nonna know how bad things were going for me."

"You could have written to *me*."

"I wasn't sure you'd want to hear from me. I didn't know what to say." He lifted his gaze. "Okay, I didn't want you to know how bad things were either."

Finally, the truth? "How did you survive?"

He rubbed the back of his neck. "I'd saved some money working for Doc Tilbert. I used that to buy food, slept under bridges, headed south before winter… When I ran out of money, I hired out to do odd jobs."

"What kind of jobs?"

"Almost anything. At least, people usually trusted me. I met runaways who had to steal or worse to keep body and soul together."

"Were you afraid?"

"All the time."

"Did you miss home at all?" *Did you miss me?*

"A lot…surprisingly."

"Then why didn't you come home?" She squinted at him, waiting for an answer.

"I don't know." He frowned as if rethinking. "Nobody needed me here. Maybe I had to figure out I was worth something before I could come back."

"You were always worth something, Tony."

He gave her a doubtful little smile. "Thanks, but that's not what I felt inside."

How could she argue with him about something as personal as his own self-worth? "How did you figure it all out?"

"I don't know."

"You don't want to tell me."

He rubbed the back of his neck. "In Memphis, I started hanging out with some guys who'd been on the streets for a while…you know, to learn the ropes. And I figured safety in numbers, right?"

She nodded.

"It worked for a while, but in the end, they beat me up and threatened to kill me. But while they argued over my stash of food and meager belongings, I managed to get away. I hid under a bridge all night, afraid to fall asleep in case they hunted me down."

Tears stung her eyes. Her heart feeling as if it might break, she grasped his hand. "What did you do?"

"Moved on to Atlanta the next morning, kept my guard up and relied only on myself. I learned when soup kitchens and shelters were open and made sure I was first in line. Somehow, I got through."

"Thank God." Maggie swiped at her tears.

"I didn't see a lot of Him on the streets."

"Who ran the soup kitchens and shelters?"

"I get your point."

"Do you remember that Bible verse…'Come to me,

all you who are weary and burdened, and I will give you rest'?"

"Sure. But it's pretty hard to rest when survival is your main concern."

"After my parents died, I learned surviving isn't just up to us, Tony. Sometimes, resting in Him was the only way I could survive."

"Also hard to remember on the streets."

As difficult as it was to know how bad it had been for him, she was grateful he had opened up to her. Like he used to. "Thank you for telling me."

He peered into her eyes. "Who else would I tell?" He dropped his gaze and reached to grasp her locket, his rough fingers brushing her throat.

Oh, no. Why had she worn the necklace this morning? *Please don't let him open the locket.*

"I'm surprised you kept this."

"It was a birthday gift." She sounded almost as panicked as she felt. "Why wouldn't I keep it?"

"Oh, I don't know…maybe because you didn't want to be reminded of me." He flipped open the locket and looked at the pictures inside.

Maggie's heart almost stopped. The pictures—one of her parents, one of him and the tiny picture of their baby girl. Would he want to know who the baby was? Was she ready to tell him?

"You were a cute baby."

She swallowed. He assumed the baby was her?

"Who's the skinny guy?"

Maggie dragged a shallow breath. "An old friend."

He raised an eyebrow. "Do you still count me as a friend?"

"Maybe."

"But friends say goodbye." Snapping the locket

closed, he withdrew his hand. "I was afraid you'd talk me out of leaving."

She nodded. "I would have tried."

"I couldn't risk it. Not even when I knew I would hurt you by leaving that way. I'm sorry, Maggie. I just hope you can forgive me someday."

She caught her breath. She'd waited ten long years for his apology. And now that he'd said it, it didn't change anything.

But that didn't stop her from drinking in his words like parched earth drinks in rain. Returning his dark gaze, she felt as if her heart was melting.

I know what You would have me do, God. You don't want me to hang on to this burden anymore. "I forgive you, Tony," she whispered.

Tony was all thumbs in Nonna's old kitchen. Somehow, cooking the spaghetti and marinara sauce he'd made a thousand times before had become a monumental task with Maggie bustling around setting the table and searching the pantry and cupboards for things he needed. She clearly didn't know her way around Nonna's kitchen any better than he did.

But that hadn't been the real problem.

The real problem was that food was the last thing on Tony's mind. Even now as he sat at the table with Maggie and Hannah chatting about something or other that had happened at the diner today, his appetite had deserted him. That never happened.

But he just couldn't seem to wrap his mind around what had happened in the attic with Maggie. She'd forgiven him for leaving.

How? Why? He still had a hard time believing it. Of course, he hadn't known how to respond. Still didn't.

She must be on pretty good footing with God to have found enough strength to forgive him.

"This is delicious." Maggie blissfully rolled her eyes and concentrated on twisting spaghetti around her fork.

"It's terrific," Hannah agreed as she plopped another forkful into her mouth.

"Thanks." He pushed food around on his plate. Trouble was, knowing Maggie would never forgive him for leaving the way he did had seemed to keep a barrier between them. A barrier that meant her friendship was more than he deserved. Which was true, and he'd accepted that.

"Stella would enjoy this marinara sauce so much, Tony." Maggie smiled.

Her smile making his mouth go dry, he quickly looked away. Apparently, he'd counted on that barrier being there to remind him how to respond to her smile.

"You could take some to the rehab center for her," Maggie suggested.

Tony glanced at her, then away again. He couldn't help feeling awkward with her. Uncomfortable. He didn't know how to relate to her now that she'd forgiven him. Now, he couldn't be sure of the parameters of their relationship. Was that the problem?

"I'll look for a small container after supper if you want." She dabbed her mouth with her napkin.

"You missed a spot." He pointed.

"Oh?" She moved her napkin everywhere and still managed to miss the splotch of spaghetti on her chin. She looked at him expectantly. "Gone?"

He shook his head. "Lower."

With a huff, she handed him the napkin.

His throat going completely dry, he took the napkin and slowly, carefully wiped away the smudge of sauce.

She met his eyes. "Thanks."

He wanted to pound his head against the table. How could she act as if nothing had changed since she'd gone and forgiven him? Didn't she know she'd left him floundering around in territory he had no clue how to navigate?

"You want to go to church tomorrow morning with Hannah and me?" Maggie asked.

"Church?" He frowned at her.

She nodded. "You used to spend a lot of time there, remember?"

"Long time ago," he murmured.

"Aren't you curious? At least, a little bit?"

He shrugged. "Maybe."

"Then come with us. I sing in the choir, so you can sit with Hannah and keep her company."

"I hate sitting by myself," Hannah admitted.

Maggie gave him a pleading look.

What could he say? She'd managed to find it in her heart to forgive him for deserting her. And she was finally asking him to do something for her? How could he refuse? "Okay."

Maggie's lovely face broke into a grin. "Fantastic."

He'd clearly surprised her by agreeing to go to church with her. But her beautiful grin told him a whole lot more.

It told him that he felt as stripped and vulnerable with her as he'd ever been.

Sunday morning, Maggie swallowed her last bite of toast just as Tony walked into the kitchen. He was clean-shaven, his hair still wet from a shower. He wore a blue T-shirt and newer jeans, a summer-weight black sports jacket dangling from one finger, obviously his concession to accompanying her and Hannah to church. He looked fantastic, if not the least bit happy.

"Morning," he said a little self-consciously.

"Hi," Hannah chirped.

"Good morning," Maggie said. "Looking good. Do you want toast?"

"No, thanks. Do I have time to make coffee?"

Checking her watch, Maggie shook her head. "Maybe instant in the microwave?"

"Never mind, I'll get some later."

Hannah hopped up, transferred her cereal bowl to the sink and headed for the stairs. "I'll be right back."

"We have to get a move on. We'll meet you in the car." Maggie hustled to the sink with her teacup.

"Is the eight-thirty service crowded?" Tony asked.

Maggie gave him a wary look. Was he going to change his mind about going? She hoped not, but she wouldn't be totally surprised if he did. "It's full of the younger crowd. Many of the older people go to the later, more traditional one."

He gave a nod.

She picked up her purse off the counter. "Ready?"

"Sure." He followed her out the door, and they silently walked to the Suburban and got in.

Hannah ran down the walk, jumped in and they were off without a minute to spare. At least Tony hadn't bolted. In eight minutes flat, Maggie walked nervously up the church steps between Hannah and Tony. He was still with them, but he was as skittish as she'd ever seen him.

"Good morning." Mrs. Chandler handed them church bulletins. "It's nice to see all of you. Welcome home, Tony."

He gave a reluctant nod. "Thanks."

Maggie suppressed her anxiety, knowing Tony's reluctance to call Noah's Crossing home. "Any news from Jess?"

Mrs. Chandler's face melted in a smile. "She's decided to take a class toward finishing her interior-design degree now that Jake's thriving in play school two mornings a week."

"Great." Maggie grinned. "I need to call her and catch up."

"You do that, dear. You know how much she looks forward to talking to you."

"I enjoy it, too." Maggie led the way into the sanctuary, then turned to Tony. "Do you want to sit near the back?"

"Not here." Tony glowered down at her. "I don't want to sit by Coach Benton. Let's move up a little."

"Okay. You and Hannah can decide where you want to sit. I need to be with the choir."

Tony's jaw clenching, he glanced around as if looking for the least threatening spot in the entire church.

Maggie touched his arm.

He looked down at her, his eyes pinched, defensive.

"Relax, okay?" She gave him a smile of encouragement. "This is a peaceful place. Just try to focus on the service and not worry about the people."

"I'll try."

"Good." She turned to Hannah. "I'll meet you at the car afterward."

Hannah's eyes rounded in surprise. "No doughnuts this morning?"

"Not this morning." She had the distinct impression Fellowship Hour might be a tad too much for Tony. Maggie hustled front and left to join her fellow choir members just as Betsy Carmichael began playing the prelude.

Seated, she sorted through her music to be sure her sheets were in the right order, then scanned the congregation for Tony and Hannah. She found them near the middle, Hannah seated next to Lucas and his grandmother, Tony beside her on the center aisle. He had his head down, looking through the bulletin. So far as Maggie could tell, he was surrounded by people he shared no past with. Good. Maybe he'd be able to relax and enjoy the service.

Betsy transitioned her tempo, the powerful organ swelling in powerful strains of "Joyful, Joyful, We Adore Thee." Maggie stood along with the choir and the rest of the congregation and joined in singing the delightful hymn.

Recognizing Tony's rich bass in the sea of singers sent goose bumps dancing over her skin. It had been so long since she'd heard him sing, and she'd always loved it.

A couple hurrying down the aisle caught her eye. Sheriff and Mrs. Bunker were often last-minute arrivers. People moved over to allow them room, and they shuffled into the pew directly behind Tony and Hannah.

Oh, no. Not there. Tony's worst nightmare. Maggie almost lost her place in her favorite hymn. *Please, God, don't let Tony turn around.*

"Joyful, joyful, we adore Thee," Tony sang with gusto. He liked this hymn. He especially liked hearing Maggie's clear, melodic soprano ringing true through others' voices. Her tone was richer and more trained now than it had been in her teenage years, but it was just as engrossing. He couldn't help smiling at her through the crowd.

She returned his smile, then suddenly, her smile was gone. In its place, she looked alarmed, unhappy. What was wrong? She seemed to be focusing behind him. He turned to see what or who had stolen her smile.

And looked directly into the sullen face of Sheriff Bunker.

Without blinking or missing a note, Tony turned front and center, his mind racing to weigh his alternatives. Walking out would feel really good right about now. He could make a statement to Bunker by walking out. And he wouldn't have to sit through the entire service pretending the sheriff wasn't breathing down his neck. He turned to leave.

But would Bunker get it? Probably not. He'd never been the brightest bulb in the pack. And walking out would confuse Hannah and upset Maggie. Not a good trade-off.

Hearing the hymn ending, he scrapped the idea of leaving and sat. He tried to put Bunker out of his mind. He needed to settle down and concentrate on the service like Maggie had suggested. But in truth, he figured he might just as well resign himself to fifty-five more minutes of wishing he was anyplace else on earth.

The choir's parts were Tony's favorite times. Maggie sang alone, in a duet or in groups, her lovely voice both uplifting and hauntingly serene.

The service continued to move quickly. After a short prayer, a teenage boy gave a brief children's sermon, kids filed out of the church and teenagers gave the readings. The congregation sang a hymn praising God, then the preacher stepped to the pulpit.

Ah…the sermon. Tony braced himself for the ultimate lecture. If memory served him, the theme would focus on denying everything that was humanly possible and trying to convince him to be somebody he could never be, no matter how hard he tried.

But unlike sermons in his past, this one wasn't filled with accusation and condemnation. Instead, the pastor's tone was light, empathetic and imbued with hope. His words were direct. His message was to the point. And he clearly reflected the freshness of the entire worship service.

He pointed out that souls need communion with God beyond all other needs. That He wants us to know Him, to come to one with Him. That prayer is His way to accomplish that.

Wow. Tony needed time to reflect on the powerful words. Like, maybe, for the rest of his life.

Maggie and the choir sang a beautiful song that carried Tony's spirit soaring along with it. When it ended, he managed to retrieve his wallet from his back pocket and put some bills in the offering plate being passed by the usher in the center aisle.

Turning to see Hannah's sweet smile for Lucas, Tony directed his gaze to Maggie's face.

She shot him a question with her eyes.

Was she concerned about his response to the service? Or the sheriff? Probably the former, knowing Maggie. Swallowing against a ton of emotions he had yet to figure out what to do with, about church and about her, he gave her a thumbs-up.

Her smile lit her whole face.

Suddenly, the unmistakable thought that he wanted more than friendship with her hit him solidly between the eyes.

Come on, Stefano. Get real. You have no business thinking about a deeper relationship with her.

She was an amazing, independent, talented woman with a heart as big as God's universe. She was forced to grow up fast when her parents died, and she'd done a remarkable job of pulling her life together. And someday, she needed a guy who'd settle down and be there for her.

Did that sound like him? Not by a long shot.

Chapter Seven

Tony held the convenience store's glass door for Maggie, then walked into the air-conditioning behind her. He headed for the long line of coolers in the back, ignoring the man behind the counter and his customer. The farther Tony could steer clear of citizens from the past, the better.

Going to church with Maggie and Hannah this morning had been a whole lot more mingling than he'd planned with Noah's Crossing's finest while he was here. Managing to avoid Sheriff Bunker after the service had taken special ingenuity. But keeping his focus on the service and off the people had made the experience serene, peaceful, even inspiring. When he'd said as much to Maggie, she'd somehow refrained from saying she'd told him so.

And now, she had asked him to help her hang posters in town. Not exactly his cup of joe, but he couldn't help being pleased she'd asked him for something he could deliver. His helping her with one of her projects was kind of like old times. Or it would be if he could get his teasing "old times" footing back with her.

"Hey, Keith," Maggie greeted cheerily. "Is it okay if

I tack a poster for the Church Benefit Dairy Breakfast on your bulletin board?"

"Go right ahead, Maggie." The warmth in the older man's voice was unmistakable.

Reaching into the cooler for a six-pack of cola, Tony heard the door open and close, probably the other customer leaving.

"Harold and Louise Phillips hosting the breakfast again this year?" Keith asked.

"Yes," Maggie answered. "It promises to be bigger and better than ever. Channel Nine is covering it. Have you signed up to do a display?"

"Nope. I wouldn't miss that good food, though."

"Great. How's Stacy doing with her summer college classes?" Maggie asked.

Walking toward the front of the store, Tony frowned. Little Stacy Meyers?

"Good, far as I know. We don't see much of her because she goes to bed with the chickens. And gets up with them to help Della out with her baking in the wee hours before going to class."

Tony set the cola on the counter. "Stacy's old enough to go to college?"

The slender man in the light blue shirt and thinning sandy hair grinned. "She's nineteen. I can hardly believe it myself."

"When she graduated last year, she won the Clarissa Chandler four-year scholarship to study science," Maggie interjected.

"Good for her." Tony remembered Nonna writing about Jessie's sister dying in a fire.

"I used to babysit her," Maggie said from near the front door. "Boy, did she love ice cream."

Keith chuckled. "She still has a serious sweet tooth, but she doesn't gain an ounce. She works too hard."

Tony fished his wallet out of his back jeans pocket.

"I think Stacy's genes have a lot to do with her not gaining weight," Maggie said, pinning her poster. "Keith hasn't put on a pound in ten years, has he, Tony?"

"Guess not." Tony did a quick scan of the man behind the counter as he handed him a few bills.

Keith rang up the sale and gave Tony change. "You've put on some solid muscle since I last saw you."

"Heavy construction."

Keith gave a nod. "Do you need more tacks, Maggie?"

"There are plenty here. I'm just catching up on the news."

Tony picked up his purchase, ready to leave old-home week behind.

"How's your grandma doing, Tony?"

He paused and met Keith's eyes, expecting to see curiosity. But he could swear concern was what he saw. "She's hanging in there."

"She's a good woman. Give her my best."

"I'll do that."

Keith smiled. "And welcome home."

Tony decided not to enlighten the man on his views about Noah's Crossing. He strode to Maggie, who was stretching on tiptoe to read the top announcements posted on the bulletin board. She looked about nineteen herself with her copper curls tied back in one of those scrunchie things. He wondered what she'd been like at nineteen.

Where had he been then? Cambodia? Laos? It didn't really matter. He'd missed out on a lot of her growing up, and he couldn't help wishing he hadn't. He stopped behind her and looked at her colorful poster. "Looks good."

"Thanks." She waved at Keith. "See you. Tell Stacy hi."

"Sure thing," Keith replied.

Tony held the door for Maggie, then walked beside her to the Hog and opened the saddlebag.

She leaned to take out more posters. "I want to put one in Josh's Service Station and one in the diner. Maybe a few other places, too. Okay?"

"Okay." He stashed the soda in the saddlebag, latched it and reached for the helmet.

"Let's walk, okay?"

He didn't have a burning desire to hobnob with people in town. "I'll wait here."

"Oh, come on." She brushed his arm with her hand. "Walk with me."

Not having the heart to tell her that strolling up Main Street wasn't his idea of a good time, he fell in beside her. "Sounds as if this breakfast is a pretty big deal."

She flashed him a smile. "It is. You'd like it."

"Breakfast on a farm? Why would I like it?" Glancing over his shoulder at a young boy wheeling toward them on a skateboard, he clasped Maggie's elbow and guided her off the sidewalk.

"Hey, Maggie, watch this," the boy yelled, zipping by them balancing on one foot.

"Wow! That's amazing, Brett," Maggie yelled back, a laugh in her voice.

She'd so effortlessly made the boy feel important. She obviously loved kids. She had a joy and naturalness about her with them.

She stepped onto the sidewalk and turned her attention to Tony again.

He didn't seem to know what to do with it. He was having a rough time relating to her on this new level. It was difficult to tease a woman he held in awe. He let out a breath and shoved his hands in his pockets. How could he continue to pretend she was the girl he'd left behind when she'd clearly grown way beyond him? Sure, she'd always been way ahead of him, but now, he realized she had a depth of maturity about her that he didn't know how to deal with.

She peered up at him as they walked. "The breakfast is meant to promote dairy farming, and the proceeds go to funding the youth program at church. It's fun. The food is great, and everybody comes. You'd see a lot of people you know."

He raised an eyebrow. "And that's a good thing?"

"Absolutely. You sound like a hermit or something."

"Or something."

She greeted and was greeted by people of all ages on their trek down Main Street. From their exchange, you'd think she was related to all of them.

After putting a poster in The Chocolate Nugget, they angled across the small parking lot alongside the new service station with the false front. It was a little too clean, a little too perfect. Tony had been going to the one on the other end of town near the rehab center that really had been there forever.

Maggie waved at the big man in navy pants and shirt near the gas pumps who was cleaning the windshield on an impressive-looking steel-gray Escalade.

Tony admired the vehicle for a minute, the smell of gasoline reassuring. Perfect or not, a filling station was still a filling station.

"Is it okay if I put a poster for the Dairy Breakfast in your window?" Maggie asked the man at the pumps.

"Go ahead. There's tape in the top right-hand drawer in my desk. Help yourself." The trust and affection in the man's tone was there just as it had been in Keith Meyers's voice.

"Thanks." She smiled up at Tony. "Do you recognize him?"

Tony studied the man, his movements more familiar than anything else about him. "Josh Craven?"

"Sure is." Maggie headed for the garage door. "I'll see you in a couple minutes," she called over her shoulder.

Looked like Josh was doing well for himself. He and Tony had butted heads for the same positions in sports all through school. Josh hadn't been any good either. Tony strode over to the pumps.

Josh gave Tony a fleeting frown that ended in a grin. "Tony Stefano. I heard you were back in town."

Of course he had. Tony shook Josh's hand. "Looks like you have a thriving operation here."

"I do okay. Noah's Crossing is getting a second wind since we were kids," Josh said.

"Seems that way."

"You home for long?"

Home again. "A few days."

"Give me a call. I work a lot of hours, but maybe we can set up a time to get together and catch up." Josh hurried off to attend to a red Mercedes.

The owners of these late-model cars in town probably lived in those upscale houses on Doc Tilbert's old farm. As for getting together with Josh, it probably wouldn't work out. He had only a few more days here.

Maggie walked to meet him, throwing a wave Josh's way. "Thank you."

Too bad Tony couldn't bottle all that sunshine and goodwill and take it back to South America with him. They continued up the street past an empty lot where Tony, Josh and a bunch of guys used to play pickup baseball. The grass was long now. "Kids must have found a better place to play ball."

"There's more going on in town. Kids don't seem to have much time to just hang out anymore."

"We learned a lot just hanging out."

"We did, didn't we?" Maggie gave him a smile. "And we had lots of fun, too."

He nodded in agreement.

Passing Sarah's Drugs and Gifts, Maggie held up her poster to the woman who'd just turned the sign in the window over to read Closed.

The woman smiled and pointed to a similar poster in her plateglass window, then held up her hand to indicate they should wait while she hurried to the door, pulled it open and flew down the steps to meet them. "I was about to call you, Maggie."

"Sarah Taylor, you remember Tony?"

"Sure do." Sarah smiled. "I saw you in church this morning. Welcome home."

Whatever. He nodded politely. "Thanks."

Sarah turned her attention to Maggie. "I wanted to tell you that Senator Benson's wife stopped in the store today with a woman I didn't recognize. They were deep in conversation about you and your roses the entire time they shopped. I thought you'd want to know."

Maggie smiled. "I'm working on a plan for a rose garden for the Bensons. Thanks for the feedback."

"Sure. Good to see you, Tony." Sarah turned to her store.

"Same here." He fell into step alongside Maggie again. They passed the bank, its outrageous architecture sticking out like a sore thumb, and headed for the diner.

Maggie jogged up the steps.

He opened the door for her, then followed her into the hubbub. Apparently, they hadn't entirely missed dinner hour.

Several tables were empty, but the counter was crowded, customers calling out and waving to them... well, to Maggie. He wanted to turn and wait for her outside, but no doubt, she'd frown on that idea.

The smell of roast beef mixing with delicious baked goods made his mouth water even though he had already eaten. Della had always made great food. And he had to admit the place was brighter and more lively than it had been when he was a kid.

Della hurried by, a plate of pie in each hand. "Hannah's in back washing dishes."

Maggie nodded and held up her poster. "May I put this in your window?"

Della's jovial, fifty-something face lit up. "It's beautiful, Maggie. You're a good artist. I still remember when your mother used to bring you in here with posters you'd made for one of your causes. She was so proud."

Maggie looked pleased.

"I'll be right back." Della hustled away to deliver the plates of pie.

Turning to the counter, Tony's focus narrowed on broad shoulders in a tan sheriff's uniform. Sheriff Bunker again. The last person on earth Tony wanted to see, and he'd managed to run into him twice in one day. How lucky could he get?

The sheriff spun his stool and stood, his waistline thicker than it had been, but the officious, I've-got-your-number expression was just as blatant as ever. "Tony Stefano."

"Sheriff."

Bunker made for the door.

Same old sheriff, much too small a man to make an apology for wrongly accusing him. Tony tried to shrug it off.

"Tony Stefano?"

He turned.

"Clyde Billings from the lumberyard. Welcome home." Clyde stuck out his hand.

Tony shook it. If he remembered right, Maggie used to call Clyde the Tin Woodman because of his kind heart.

"How's your grandma?"

"Hanging in there."

"Good to hear. Tell her hello."

Tony gave a nod.

"Good to see ya." Clyde clapped him on the shoulder, turned and walked over to sit at a table.

Della zoomed behind the counter. "I have a fresh raspberry pie left. Stella's favorite."

"I'll take it," Tony decided.

Della hurried to take a pie from the display case and began wrapping it with experienced hands. "Put your poster right there, Maggie. I'll tape it in the window by the door so everybody can see it."

"Thank you." Maggie set the poster near the cash register.

Tony peeled a twenty from his wallet and laid it on the counter.

Della handed the wrapped pie to him. Giving him a warm smile, she picked up the cash and handed it back. "Tell Stella I said hi and let her know I'm thinking of her."

He frowned. "I will, but I want to pay for the pie."

"Keep your money, Tony. I'm just so glad you came home to see your nonna."

Sweeping the counter with his gaze, he spotted a jar announcing Feed the Hungry. He took the bill from Della's outstretched hand and plopped it into the jar.

Della's smile broadened. "A man after my own heart."

"Thanks for the pie." He hoped he sounded grateful. Truth was, he was irritated and confused, and he didn't know why. He opened the door for Maggie, and they headed for the convenience store where they'd left the Harley.

"Can't accept a gift even when it's for Stella?" Maggie mused.

"All I ever wanted from this town was a fair shake."

Maggie stared at him, eyebrows dipping in confusion. "Not following."

"It's just that…when I was a kid…" Tony searched for words to describe what he was feeling and came up empty. "I don't know what I'm trying to say."

"You're thinking about Sheriff Bunker, aren't you?"

Tony let out a derisive laugh. "He sure hasn't changed. He probably still thinks I hit Doc Tilbert on the head and stole his money. Unbelievable." The memory of those long-ago accusations still made him sick to his stomach. Working for the doctor had made him feel strong, useful, needed. All the things he'd desperately wanted back then. All the things a boy needed to feel.

"He knows you didn't do it. You know he arrested Danny Judd, don't you?" Maggie brushed his arm in a comforting gesture.

And it would have been comforting before she forgave him. Now, he couldn't deny he wanted it to mean more than that. Too bad he'd thrown away that privilege when he'd left town. "Yeah, Nonna told me in her letters."

Maggie nodded. "The sheriff just doesn't want to admit he was wrong about you. But the rest of the town never felt that way. You must have picked up how happy they are to see you. Keith and Josh and Clyde. And, of course, Della."

"But I never wanted handouts."

"Della didn't give you a handout. She gave a pie to Stella."

Of course, Maggie was right. But then why did he still feel this way? Almost as if he was a kid again, dependent on others with no one needing him. Not entirely true. Doc Tilbert had needed him. He shook his head, suddenly conscious of Maggie still watching him with concern in her eyes. "I'm okay."

"You sure? We can talk about it. Maybe I can help."

He was about to say he didn't want her help but bit his tongue. It might be true, but a comment like that would only hurt her. And if he knew anything, he knew she was one person he never wanted to hurt again. "The town sure is fond of you."

She eyed him as if suspicious of his change of topic, but a smile tweaked the corners of her lips despite her skepticism. "And I'm quite fond of the town."

"Out of curiosity, is there anybody in Noah's Crossing you don't know?"

"I don't know all the new people."

"I'll bet you know a good percentage of them."

"I've done landscaping for a lot of them. And some are active in church. But I have a soft spot for the people who knew my parents. When they talk about my dad's practical jokes or Mom's great fudge bottom pie, it helps. I love that so many people remember them."

"They've all adopted you."

She turned to him, a smile breaking free. "That's so sweet, Tony. I like that idea."

"You really belong here."

"Yes," she said softly. "So do you."

"I've never belonged anywhere."

"Have you ever wanted to?"

"Never," he answered unequivocally. But the hollow feeling in his gut called him a liar.

The next afternoon, Maggie looked down at the top of Stella's pink sun hat and carefully maneuvered the wheelchair around a bump in the sidewalk in front of the rehabilitation center. Jim had suggested a short walk in the sunshine might cheer up Stella.

Maggie could use some sunshine herself. She'd been cooped up in meetings with clients and potential new clients all day. But the more contracts she had, the better her chance of meeting her pressing need for money for the house. She needed to take advantage of every avenue open to her. She hesitated, but desperation won out. "Stella, I really think you should consider using the money in the cookie jar to fix the roof."

Stella shook her head. "I will not live on charity. Not Anthony's. Nor yours."

"But it's not charity. You raised Tony, you took me in, and we're both very grateful to you. Please let us help."

"You help me every day, dear. But I don't want your money or Anthony's."

Maggie wasn't surprised by Stella's attitude, but it meant she was no closer to figuring out how to get the money she needed. And she wasn't cheering Stella up either, was she? She scanned her mind to think of a way to do that. Stella always enjoyed hearing about Maggie's work. "This morning, I met with Senator Benson's wife. She wants me to design a rose garden for their beautiful new vacation home on Rainbow Lake."

"A rose garden sounds lovely. I miss my roses."

Roses. An even better way to engage Stella. "The Salvatore roses are heavy with buds almost ready to open."

Stella reached back to pat Maggie's hand on the wheelchair handle. "Salvatore never knew he had bred the perfect rose, but the one I named for him comes very close to perfection." Stella sniffed, a sure sign tears were gathering in her eyes. Tears she would deny.

Maggie's heart swelled with love for her old friend. "The arbor is in full bloom. And the yellow climbers on the front porch are magnificent."

"My Salvatore's roses are his heart and mine."

"Yes," Maggie agreed, an idea beginning to take shape in her mind. Could Stella's roses possibly be the answer to her money problems? They would sell like hotcakes to a world of rose enthusiasts waiting for the attributes these possessed—especially the Salvatore.

But the roses didn't belong to Maggie. Before she entertained thoughts of selling them, she needed to feel

Stella out. "Did Salvatore ever consider marketing his roses?"

"They made us happy only. I want you to have them, dear. They're my legacy to you for loving me as a daughter all these years. I had this put in my will."

Maggie couldn't think about Stella's will. She wouldn't. She stopped the wheelchair. Careful to avoid her friend's supported leg, she bent and wrapped her arms around Stella's thin shoulders. "You're not going to need a will. Not anytime soon."

"I'm very old, Maggie. Very tired."

Stella's words and tone set off an alarm in Maggie's mind. She needed to help her see the positive again. Give her a reason to hold on. "You need rest. And you have to do your therapy. Then you'll get healthy and strong enough to work in your gardens again."

"That would be lovely, dear...." Stella looked listlessly off to the horizon.

Swallowing her alarm, Maggie kissed her friend's weathered cheek, straightened and began pushing the wheelchair again. She had to bring Stella home soon.

But she had no right to do that without Tony's approval, and he would never agree unless she had the house fixed up first. How was she going to get the money she needed for repairs? "Stella...maybe your roses could pay for repairs to the house. Especially the Salvatore. I've never seen a rose that compares with its classic floribunda style and constant blooming."

"But there have been so many excellent roses developed over the years."

"Not any that have that coral-pink color and spicy scent. Plus it's hardy enough for Wisconsin winters."

"I would be proud if you choose to share the roses with the world, just as Salvatore would be proud."

Maggie couldn't help being excited about the idea. Selling the roses might also give Stella something to look forward to. She mulled over what she'd need to do to bring the rose to market. "We'll apply for patents. And I'll contact the American Nurserymen's Association to find out how to go about entering the All-America competitions. Winning the competition is the surest way to announce a great rose to the world. And the Salvatore is a great one." Realizing she was pushing Stella too fast, she slowed her pace.

Stella turned stiffly to peer up at her. "But you must not worry too much, dear. Worry is not good."

Maggie nodded. Once she got Stella back home where she belonged, she'd stop worrying. Until then, worry and she seemed to be attached at the hip. *Please help me put things in Your hands.*

"Anthony brought spaghetti with marinara sauce for my lunch today."

"That's wonderful, Stella. He's a very accomplished cook, don't you think?"

"Yes, he is." Stella sighed. "He's a little heavy-handed with the garlic for my taste, though."

Maggie closed her eyes for a second. Poor Tony. Stella had probably shared her observation with him. "But he was very thoughtful to bring Italian food for you."

"Of course he was. He told me he built a fire in the wildflower meadow." Stella glanced back at Maggie, concern in her expression. "He said he made you unhappy."

Maggie's blood pressure began rising just thinking about the beautiful flowers crumpling in the heat. But he'd told Stella? He must have been searching hard for things to talk about. "He destroyed part of the patch of blue false indigo. They were in full bloom."

"Prairie plants are resilient as long as their deep roots are not damaged. Wait and watch. Perhaps we will see new shoots next spring."

Stella was planning for next spring? That eased Maggie's mind a bit. And she'd forgotten…she had good news she hadn't shared yet, news that would make Stella happy. "Tony apologized for leaving the way he did. And God helped me forgive him."

"Oh, my dear." Stella reached up for Maggie to grasp her hand. "I'm so happy for you. 'Forgiveness is to set a prisoner free, and to realize the prisoner was you.'"

Tears blurred Maggie's vision. "Yes," she whispered. "I can't remember where that quote is from, can you?"

"Corrie ten Boom wrote it."

"Oh, yes. The woman who forgave her captors after she was released from a Nazi prison camp."

"Yes. And does this mean you are considering telling Anthony about the baby?"

Maggie's heart ached. "I don't think so."

"You don't believe he has a right to know?"

"He does have a right to know, but knowing will hurt him. And he can't do anything to change the past. He'll be here such a short time. I'm afraid he'll wish he had never come back."

"Are you afraid he'll blame you for giving the baby away?"

Was she? "Maybe. And I'm afraid he'll blame himself. Do you think I should tell him, Stella?"

"I do. But you must do what you believe is right, and trust Anthony to do what he must, as well."

That's what worried her. He'd always hated Noah's Crossing because he'd wanted so much to be with his father. If she told him about the baby, he'd have one more reason to hate it here.

What could he do if he knew his leaving and staying away had cost him his child? Nothing.

Telling him would be just plain cruel.

Chapter Eight

Tony parked the Harley alongside Maggie's Suburban in her greenhouse parking lot and headed for the door. On his way back from an important run to the store, he'd taken a quick tour of the housing development on Doc Tilbert's farm and ridden away with a solution to Maggie and Nonna's housing problem.

Making sure they'd be safe and comfortable and as worry-free as possible was the least he could do before he left Noah's Crossing. He was fired up to tell Maggie about it. He reached for the door.

A slender brunette in jeans and a yellow blouse emerged. "Well, hello."

He frowned, wondering if the woman was somebody he should recognize from the past.

The brunette gave him an appraising smile and stuck out her hand. "I'm Leah, Maggie's friend, old college roommate and current accountant. You must be Tony."

He shook her hand. "That's me. Nice to meet you."

"Same here." She flashed him a friendly smile. "Maggie's in the back."

"Thanks."

"Off to do an errand." Leah turned and glided across the parking lot.

Nice. But she didn't do a thing for him. She didn't have brown eyes or copper hair, and she was definitely missing Maggie's depth and don't-mess-with-me attitude.

He closed the door, the smells of damp earth rich and fragrant. Humid air enveloping him, he peered down dim aisles between rows and rows of plants. "Hey, Maggie," he yelled, his voice echoing loudly off the glass walls enclosing the giant structure.

Two seconds tops, she appeared at the other end of one of the long aisles, unsettled as a bird rousted from its nest. She wore blue-and-white-striped bib overalls cut off above her knees, a white T-shirt and bare feet. And he was much happier to see her than he had any right to be.

"What's the matter? Did something happen with Stella?" Her eyes wide with alarm, she rubbed at her dirt-covered hands with a towel.

"I took her lunch. Things seemed okay, but her taste buds were off. She told me there was too much garlic in my marinara sauce. What's with that? She could never get enough garlic."

Maggie threw her hands in the air in one of her trademark gestures. "Is that why you're yelling as if the sky is falling?"

"Your accountant said you were working in the back."

"You met Leah?"

"Yup."

"She's been wanting to meet you." She dropped the dirt-smeared towel on a bench. "So you stopped for a grand tour of my new greenhouse?"

He glanced around, anxious to tell her about his idea, but he guessed it would keep long enough for a quick tour. "Uh, sure, I'd love to see your greenhouse."

"Do you have an hour to spare?"

An hour? What could take an hour to look at in a greenhouse?

She rolled her eyes. "Don't look so horrified. For you, a ten-minute tour."

He gave her an apologetic grin. What could he say? Plants and greenhouses weren't usually among his favorite things. But she, no doubt, knew that.

She proved to be a woman of her word. Ten minutes later, she'd impressed him with her state-of-the-art misting system, her timed, artificial lights designed to compensate for Wisconsin's long winters, her potting benches and her jungle of plants. She'd spouted off their Latin names as if they were old friends.

Not that he could remember a single one. But he got a real kick out of the pride in her manner. No question, she loved what she did. She was as animated as a kid showing off, and her enthusiasm was contagious. Problem was, he'd had to remind himself a couple times not to reach out and grasp her hand. What was up with that?

"That's it for the greenhouse," Maggie announced. "The rest of my forty acres is planted in perennials and shrubs and ornamental trees. Except for the woods."

He hoped she didn't plan to give him a tour of her entire forty acres. But if she did, she did. And he'd probably enjoy every minute.

She led him into a cramped back room crowded with supplies stacked around two desks. "This is my office." She thumped her hand on one of the desks and pointed to the other. "That's Leah's. We run a no-frills operation."

"I can see that." He had as much room in his make-shift offices on building sites. But finally, he could tell her why he'd stopped in. "I took a tour of Doc's old farm this morning."

"Oh? Did you recognize the terrain in spite of the houses covering it now?"

"For the most part. I missed a few of my favorite trees, though."

She nodded in understanding. "So you're visiting your past haunts? Do you want to see the tree house?"

He met her eyes. "The tree house?"

"Or not." Flushing, she dropped her gaze as if re-thinking her offer.

He rubbed the back of his neck. He was curious about the tree house, but… "Uh, sure…why not?"

She squinted up at him? "Yeah?"

He nodded.

Turning, she padded ahead of him, stopping near the door to slip into a pair of beat-up clogs before she led the way outside, locked the door and stomped across the gravel parking lot ahead of him.

The house where she and her parents had lived stood nearby, looking the same as it had when they were kids. "Do you rent out your house?"

She shook her head.

"What do you use it for, then?"

"Nothing. It's empty."

"If you don't want to rent it out, why don't you convert it into offices with a conference room and employee break room?"

"Very resourceful."

"Thanks." But her tone told him he'd better not hold his breath for that to happen. He followed her into the woods. There, the tree house stood on its four stilts, half-hidden in the giant leaves of the spreading bur oak branch that supported it.

Its weathered boards contrasted with the newness of the wooden ladder leaning against the tree limb outside the door. Other than looking a whole lot smaller, the place appeared exactly as he remembered it. A dull ache tightened his throat.

Maggie stepped out of her clogs and climbed the ladder. She pushed open the door and disappeared inside. By the time he'd removed his boots and wedged himself through the door, she sat on the floor, legs folded in front of her, near the shiny, open window. The sun glinted off her copper hair like a halo.

Despite the open window, the air was hot and stuffy with the scent of old wood and pine cleaner. The tiny abode was cobweb-free, the plank floor swept clean. Apparently, she still came here.

He folded himself to the floor across from her. The tightness in his throat worked its way to his chest as memories flooded him of the last time he'd been here with her. They'd been so young, so innocent, so much in love. With a mental shake of his head, he forced his mind to focus on less conflicted memories.

Like Maggie chattering about her teachers and classmates. Maggie listening to his latest crisis with Nonna or disappointment with his father. Maggie surprising him with little gifts to make up for his father failing to acknowledge his birthdays. Considerate, encouraging, caring Maggie. She was still that Maggie…only much, much more. "The place looks the same."

"You expected changes?"

Grinning, he stretched his long legs out in front of him, his socks almost brushing her knees. "We had a lot of good times growing up."

A smile warmed her face. "It's really nice to know I'm not the only one who remembers."

He was glad he'd mentioned it. Making her smile felt great.

She turned, rummaged in the wood crate under the window and held a worn dog collar out to him.

"Kip's collar," Tony said.

"He's buried in Stella's backyard. He missed you when you left. He loved you, you know."

Tony picked at a splinter in the rough plank floor. Kip had been his go-to guy, his comforter when he'd had nobody else. "I considered taking him with me, but I figured he'd have a better life here. Good choice, as it turned out. But I deserted him, too. I didn't deserve his love either."

"I don't know that anybody really deserves love, do you? I mean…I think love just is."

He raised his gaze to her face. He saw no hint of doubt in her rich brown eyes. She knew what love was. It shone bright and whole from the depths of her being. "Nonna wrote that you got engaged to a guy you met in college. What happened?"

A little frown clouded her eyes. "He graduated and got a great job in New York. I was just going into my sophomore year in college, and I wasn't interested in moving. That's what happened."

"Did you love him?" he asked tensely, realizing her answer was very important for some reason.

She nibbled her bottom lip. "I think I was more lonely than in love. Have you ever been in love, Tony?"

"Once."

"Then you know it's not an exact science. What happened?"

"You know what happened, Maggie. I left town."

She stared at him as if trying to digest his words. "You loved me?"

How could she not know? "You had to know that."

"But I told you I loved you and you said nothing."

"Would saying the words have made a difference?"

"Yes. Hearing them would have taken away some of my doubts after you left. It makes a huge difference knowing that even now."

He struggled to understand. His feelings had been so intense that it never occurred to him that she wasn't sure he loved her. "Then I'm glad I finally told you."

"So am I."

Not a clue what else to say, he desperately wanted to get back to something he knew, like buildings. But bringing up his housing idea right now seemed like a bad idea.

He shifted uncomfortably, his eyes resting on an assembly of yellowing playbills tacked to the wall, the scrawled signatures on them still visible. Backed by elaborate stage sets from different operas, youthful faces of tenors and sopranos smiled at him. He could make out his father's name, Joseph S. Stefano—principal violin, in tiny block letters near the bottom. "I can't believe you kept those posters."

Maggie's eyes widened. She was, undoubtedly, recognizing his complete change of subject. "We used to hold official hanging ceremonies after you showed the posters to your friends at school. Remember?"

"We toasted with ginger ale." He laughed, remembering their child's play, but the memory was bittersweet. "I showed up at one of his gigs after I left Noah's Crossing. I had the crazy idea that I wanted to play my trumpet for him. He seemed embarrassed to see me. I don't think anybody knew he even had a son. I left the next day."

"You deserved a better father," she said simply.

Somehow he felt better hearing her say that.

"At least you were lucky to have Stella."

"I should have made it easier for her." He shook his head.

"You were just a kid."

"An ungrateful kid. I doubt you were ever ungrateful."

She frowned. "I accepted my wonderful parents and home as if it was my due. How ungrateful was that?"

"Sounds like security to me. Secure kids are the ones who can afford to take their parents for granted. Your parents were pretty cool."

"Yes, they were."

"They seemed to get me, for some reason."

"Of course they got you." She studied him. "Where did you learn that thing about secure kids?"

"Does it make sense?"

"Amazingly."

"I have my moments."

She bit her lip, a curl falling over one eye.

He wanted to reach over and smooth it back for her, but he resisted the urge.

"After my parents died and—" She shook her head. "After my parents died, it was like I was living an awful nightmare I couldn't wake up from. When Stella brought me home with her, I went through the motions of living, but I didn't feel anything. Stella said I was afraid to feel."

He squinted at her. "It must have been awful, Maggie. How did the accident happen?"

"The roads were icy. They were on their way to see me—" She shook her head, eyes glued to the floor.

"Where were you?"

"Uh…" She pressed her hand to her throat. "I…I was staying with my mom's aunt Bea in Eau Claire."

"Over the weekend?"

She glanced up, then back at the floor. "Actually, I stayed with her my sophomore year."

"Why?"

"Uh…to help her live in her home a little while longer."

"I'm surprised your parents agreed to that in the middle of a school year."

"I attended classes…" She closed her eyes as if struggling to sort things out in her mind.

"It's okay, Maggie. You don't have to talk about that awful time."

She squeezed her eyes shut.

He gave her time to deal with her emotions. After all, the day her parents died was the worst day of her life.

"I didn't say goodbye," she whispered, tears spilling down her cheeks.

He lurched to sit beside her. He wrapped his arm around her, feeling clumsy and totally at a loss to know what to do.

She laid her head on his shoulder.

He gently stroked her hair, searching for words that might help her. "Saying goodbye wouldn't have changed anything."

"But I'd tell them I loved them. I'd hug them one last time."

He tipped her chin up and looked into her tear-filled eyes. "They knew you loved them. Everybody who saw you guys together knew. Just by the way you treated each other." He brushed away her tears, her skin unbelievably soft to his rough fingers. He didn't know what else he could say.

"Thank you."

Her words felt so good. He'd forgotten more than the fun times they'd shared as kids. He'd forgotten this, the feeling that she needed him, that she wanted him with her. And it still meant the world to him. "Do you remember the time you won the cheerleading competition and Susan Pertzborn didn't make it?"

Maggie nodded. "Second grade."

"Yeah. Susan and a couple of her loser friends taunted you on the bus and made you feel so bad, I found you up here crying."

She wiped her eyes and gave him a little smile. "You brought me a strawberry shake and made me play the 'worst-day' game with you. Your stories were so silly, I ended up in tears from laughing. You made me forget the bad stuff."

He grinned, glad she remembered his helping her feel better. He reached out and took her hand, so small in his. "Come with me now. Let me show you something really cool."

"They're so adorable," Maggie gushed. How could she help it? She stood in front of Tony, peering in the shed's small window. A shaft of sunlight spotlighted a humble cardboard box, and in that box, five feeble, newborn kittens squirmed on their mother's belly, blindly trying to nurse. A black, a gray-black tabby, two grays and a white with gray boots like its mother. "They're amazing."

"Yesterday, I stacked newspapers in that box. They weren't here then."

She stopped herself from leaning back against him. Problem was, after sharing things in the tree house that she'd never told another living soul, she felt closer to him on so many levels that it made her head swim.

He'd said he'd loved her and erased any doubt that their baby had been conceived in love. *Thank You, God. But I almost slipped about the baby. Would I have told him everything if he hadn't let me off the hook?*

"This morning, I came out to patch the hole I found in the shed, and there they all were. Good thing I put off patching that hole." He sounded as excited as a kid on Christmas morning.

"Do you think she's a feral cat?"

"I don't think so. I'm sure she can hear us, and she seems pretty relaxed, don't you think?"

"She does. Where do you think she came from?"

"Probably lost or abandoned. Or she didn't feel safe enough to have her kittens wherever she was."

"Poor thing." The idea of the mother cat having no safe place to give birth made Maggie's heart ache. She watched her tenderly lick her tiny offspring now. "I'm so glad she came here to have them."

"Pretty amazing, huh?"

She turned to look up at him and couldn't help smiling at the awe on his face. The same awe she was feeling. "Amazing," she agreed. She turned back to watch the kittens. "Do you think the mother would mind if we held them?"

"Seems kind of soon."

"You're right. We don't want to frighten her away."

His breath stirred her hair and sent a pleasant little shiver down her back. And she shouldn't be enjoying it so much.

"I didn't even know you liked cats," Maggie said.

YOUR PARTICIPATION IS REQUESTED!

Dear Reader,

Since you are a lover of inspirational romance fiction — we would like to get to know you!

Inside you will find a short Reader's Survey. Sharing your answers with us will help our editorial staff understand who you are and what activities you enjoy.

To thank you for your participation, we would like to send you 2 books and 2 gifts — **ABSOLUTELY FREE!**

Enjoy your gifts with our appreciation,

Pam Powers

SEE INSIDE FOR READER'S SURVEY

For Your Inspirational Romance Reading Pleasure...

Get 2 FREE BOOKS that feature contemporary love stories that will lift your spirits and reinforce important lessons about life, faith and love.

FREE!

We'll send you 2 books and 2 gifts
ABSOLUTELY FREE
just for completing our Reader's Survey!

YOUR READER'S SURVEY
"THANK YOU" FREE GIFTS INCLUDE:
▶ 2 Love Inspired® books
▶ 2 surprise gifts

PLEASE FILL IN THE CIRCLES COMPLETELY TO RESPOND

1) What type of fiction books do you enjoy reading? (Check all that apply)
- ○ Suspense
- ○ Inspirational Fiction
- ○ Modern-day Romances
- ○ Historical Romance
- ○ Humour
- ○ Mysteries

2) What attracted you most to the last fiction book you purchased on impulse?
- ○ The Title
- ○ The Cover
- ○ The Author
- ○ The Story

3) What is usually the greatest influencer when you <u>plan</u> to buy a book?
- ○ Advertising
- ○ Referral
- ○ Book Review

4) How often do you access the internet?
- ○ Daily
- ○ Weekly
- ○ Monthly
- ○ Rarely or never.

5) How many NEW paperback fiction novels have you purchased in the past 3 months?
- ○ 0 - 2
- ○ 3 - 6
- ○ 7 or more

YES! I have completed the Reader's Survey. Please send me the 2 FREE books and 2 FREE gifts (gifts are worth about $10) for which I qualify. I understand that I am under no obligation to purchase any books, as explained on the back of this card.

❏ I prefer the regular-print edition
105/305 IDL FMJT

❏ I prefer the larger-print edition
122/322 IDL FMJT

FIRST NAME	LAST NAME

ADDRESS

APT.#	CITY

STATE/PROV.	ZIP/POSTAL CODE

The Reader Service — Here's How It Works:
Accepting your 2 free books and 2 free gifts (gifts valued at approximately $10.00) places you under no obligation to buy anything. You may keep the books and gifts and return the shipping statement marked "cancel." If you do not cancel, about a month later we'll send you 6 additional books and bill you just $4.49 for the regular-print edition or $4.99 each for the larger-print edition in the U.S. or $4.99 each for the regular-print edition or $5.49 each for the larger-print edition in Canada. That is a savings of at least 22% off the cover price. It's quite a bargain! Shipping and handling is just 50¢ per book in the U.S. and 75¢ per book in Canada.* You may cancel at any time, but if you choose to continue, every month we'll send you 6 more books, which you may either purchase at the discount price or return to us and cancel your subscription.
*Terms and prices subject to change without notice. Prices do not include applicable taxes. Sales tax applicable in N.Y. Canadian residents will be charged applicable taxes. Offer not valid in Quebec. Books received may not be as shown. All orders subject to credit approval. Credit or debit balances in a customer's account(s) may be offset by any other outstanding balance owed by or to the customer. Please allow 4 to 6 weeks for delivery. Offer available while quantities last.

If offer card is missing write to: The Reader Service, P.O. Box 1867, Buffalo, NY 14240-1867 or visit: www.ReaderService.com

BUSINESS REPLY MAIL
FIRST-CLASS MAIL   PERMIT NO. 717   BUFFALO, NY

POSTAGE WILL BE PAID BY ADDRESSEE

THE READER SERVICE
PO BOX 1341
BUFFALO NY 14240-8571

NO POSTAGE
NECESSARY
IF MAILED
IN THE
UNITED STATES

"I didn't either. I never really got to know one until I started traveling with my foreman and his huge tabby. The Terminator."

She laughed. "The Terminator?"

"Actually, his name is George. But The Terminator and I have a working agreement. He keeps the mice under control, and I take care of the rats."

"You have a real fixation with rats, don't you?"

He laughed. "Want to help me give the mother some food and water?"

"That's what's in the mystery bag you carried down here?" She indicated the grocery bag he'd set down.

"If I'd told you what was in there, it would have spoiled my surprise."

She smiled. "It's a fantastic surprise, Tony."

He met her eyes. "Glad you like it."

"I love it," she corrected.

A grin lit up his whole face. Bending over the grocery bag, he took out a package of kibble and handed it to her, then dipped in the bag and removed a bottle of water and two heavy green plastic bowls. He handed her one of the bowls.

She set the bowl on the ground and opened the kibble. Noticing the banner on the bag, she pointed to it. "This food is for kittens, Tony."

He continued pouring the bottle of water into the other bowl. "I stopped at the vet's while I was in town. He told me to feed the mother kitten food to make sure the kittens get the right nutrition. He said he'd stop by later to check that everybody's fine."

"Good thinking." She quickly read the portion sizes on the container and poured a generous portion of kibble. "Does this look about right?"

He shrugged. "Looks good to me. Ready?"

She nodded.

He quietly opened the shed door and led the way inside. "Hi, there, little lady," he said softly. He set the bowl of water a couple feet from the box of cats.

The mother watched calmly.

Maggie set the kibble beside the water and followed Tony back outside. When she looked back, the mother was already bathing her kittens again. "She's definitely used to people."

He nodded. "I'll bring a litter box down later."

"Do you think they'll be safe here? I mean, they're so tiny, and if the mother got in that hole, predators like weasels can, too."

"If she has food, water and a litter box, she doesn't have any reason to leave the kittens while they're so helpless. But just in case, I'll put a temporary patch on the hole. She came here to keep her kittens safe, so the least we can do is help her do it, right?"

Maggie smiled. This big, strong construction guy had a real soft spot for protecting helpless creatures who needed him.

"You and Hannah will have a lot of fun socializing them so they don't grow up wild."

His comment reminded her that he would be gone. "You won't be here to watch these cute little guys grow up," she said sadly.

"You can email me pictures."

"Pictures won't be the same as your being here."

"Yeah," he said softly. "I know."

At least he didn't sound happy about leaving. That was something to be grateful for.

He rubbed the back of his neck. "You know...earlier, I mentioned I'd taken a tour of Doc Tilbert's farm?"

She nodded.

"I noticed Ideal Builders is building one-story condominiums on a cul-de-sac near the backwoods, so I stopped to check it out."

With a sinking feeling, Maggie realized what was coming and began shaking her head before he'd finished his sentence.

"It's going to be a great place, Maggie. It's affordable, owners can choose whatever level of lawn care they want, even do their own…and everything will be brand-new. No leaking roofs, no drafty windows, no hazardous electricity or ancient appliances on the verge of collapse. Any problems whatsoever, you just call maintenance."

She kept right on shaking her head. "If you think either Stella or I want to live in a sterile environment like that, you really have no clue who we are, Tony."

He squinted as if he was peering through a dense fog. "Sterile environment?"

"Stilted. Immaculate. Dead. Whatever word you want to choose."

"See, that's where you're wrong. They allow cats." He looked at her as if he'd solved one of the biggest problems of mankind.

She was so bowled over by his comment that she didn't know what to say.

"Will you come and look at it with me?"

Apparently, he'd taken her silence for acquiescence. She found her voice in a hurry. "Not interested."

He looked at her very seriously. "Maggie…we need to figure out a compromise before I go back to Brazil. If we don't, I'm going to lie awake every night worrying about what nightmare you're currently dealing with in Nonna's decrepit, old Victorian."

He was trying to take care of her? Knowing that

gave her a warm, fuzzy feeling. But would he ever understand? Laying her hand on his arm, she peered into his eyes. "I appreciate your trying to help me…I do. But how can I compromise on the house? You're conveniently forgetting that Stella's well-being is at stake."

"If Nonna ever does make it out of the rehab center—a big if from my perspective—what makes you so sure she wouldn't thrive moving to a place that would solve a bunch of problems she's been attempting to deal with for a very long time?"

Obviously, he still thought she was only being her stubborn, self-sufficient self about Stella, which meant she was still on her own, didn't it? Sadly, she withdrew her hand and trudged beside Tony to the house. "You're right about one thing, Tony. She won't make it out of the rehab center if she doesn't have her home to come back to."

Chapter Nine

Sounds of shuffling feet and muted voices came from the hall outside Nonna's room as Tony packed lunch leftovers in the cooler. Sharing his eggplant Parmesan with Nonna had proved to be a hit. No complaints about too much garlic this time.

He pulled a chair close to her bed and spread out one of the photo albums he'd brought with him. The ones he figured would be least likely to have pictures of his dad. Truth be told, he wasn't quite as confident about his blast to the past with Nonna as he'd been when he'd decided to bring the albums along.

Too bad Maggie's schedule was too full to allow her to be here to smooth troubled waters. But he'd be leaving the day after tomorrow, so there just wasn't a lot of time to wait. Besides, he'd chosen the albums carefully. He could handle this.

Things began smoothly enough. Nonna offered an occasional comment as she paged through photos of his growing-up years, countless pictures of him at various ages in assorted ragtag sports uniforms. He remembered she'd sat through some pretty bad weather sometimes to cheer him on, no matter how bad things were going between them. How had he forgotten that?

She pointed to a picture of him marching in a parade with his trumpet, wearing a band uniform she'd managed to scrounge from somebody whose kid had outgrown it. "Do you still play your trumpet?"

The trumpet he'd traded for a good meal in Arkansas? "I don't have it anymore."

"I'm sorry to hear that. You were very good."

A compliment? "Thanks." Things seemed to be going better than he could have hoped. Shots of his golden retriever were a welcome relief. And there were more pictures with friends than he'd ever remembered having. "Who took all these pictures?"

"I took some, friends gave me a few. Maggie's mother gave me many. She always had a camera in her hand, remember? She was a wonderful woman."

He nodded. "Maggie's a lot like her."

"Yes, she is."

They both chuckled at several photos of him with Maggie in all her freckled glory. Pictures of them running in the sprinkler, sitting in the apple tree outside her bedroom window, eating wands of cotton candy almost as big as she was. Several of them leaning out the window or door of her tree house.

Pigtailed or ponytailed or long curls blowing in the wind, he could almost feel the energy that still radiated from her. Could almost feel the invisible bond that still stretched between them. "Did you put the pictures in these albums, Nonna?"

"Yes. They help me relive many fond memories."

He turned her comment over in his mind. Had she forgotten all the less-than-fond ones? By the time they finished the album, Tony couldn't help noticing how tired she looked. "I'll let you get some rest now.

She shook her head. "Let's look at one more album."

"If you're tired, we can look at more pictures tomorrow," he suggested.

"One more, then I will take a nap."

She must be enjoying herself if she wanted to continue. The first few pages of the album she chose held pictures of her and Salvatore, alone or with friends of all ages.

"Do you remember him?" Nonna asked.

"I remember his booming laugh. And he let me play in the dirt in his garden. I thought that was pretty cool."

She smiled. "Salvatore loved friends and his rose garden almost as much as he loved playing with you." She turned the page and pointed to a wedding picture of Tony's parents. "So beautiful. So much in love. They met in Madrid, you know. It was Celia's first tour with her cello. They married three months later. Do you remember this picture?"

Had she forgotten? "An enlargement is still hanging on the wall in your living room."

"Yes, it is." Smiling, Nonna turned the page. "And here you are on Dolly, our gentle old horse."

"I remember her."

"Do you? You were only three when your mamma and papa brought you to visit us. You loved sitting on Dolly's back while Salvatore led you around and around the meadow."

He smiled, actually enjoying himself.

She looked pensive. "It was the only time your mamma and papa brought you home. They were very sought-after musicians, you know. Always working."

A distant memory flitted through his mind of feel-

ing second to his parents' mutual passion for each other
and their music. Another memory nudged his mind…
his father trying to turn Tony into a violin prodigy and
being sorely disappointed. Would things have been different if Tony had possessed talent for the violin? But
what was the point of wondering?

"When you were born, Salvatore and I flew to Paris
to see you. Such a sturdy baby you were. We celebrated
your first birthday with you in London, and your second
birthday in our beloved Venice. Perhaps it is no mystery
that you love to travel."

"Maybe not." For once, she wasn't blaming him for
it.

"We traveled to many performances before Salvatore's heart would no longer allow him to fly on air-
planes. When he died, your papa and mamma could not
come home."

She'd buried her husband alone? Was that the reason
she was so upset he hadn't come back for his dad's me-
morial service? Thank God, she'd had Maggie to help
her through his father's death.

She brushed a tear from her cheek. "When Salvatore died, your papa did not tell me that your beautiful
mamma was ill. They didn't want to worry me. She died
three months after Salvatore."

This was heavy stuff. "I didn't realize their deaths
were so close."

"A very sad time. Your papa struggled to go on. He
knew he could not care for you alone. That is when he
brought you to me."

"And continued with his tour," Tony said flatly.

"What else could he do, Anthony? He had contracts
to fulfill and many bills from your mamma's illness."

"But why didn't he ever come back?"

Nonna closed her eyes. "I believe he could not face the pain of coming home without his papa here. Without his beloved Celia at his side."

Tony swallowed into a tight throat. "You and I were here."

Nonna's gaze met his. "Yes."

"We should have stuck together, especially during that rough time. Isn't that what families do?"

"We hang on to God with all our strength, and we do what we can manage, Anthony. That is all we can do. You must learn to accept that."

Accept his father abandoning him because he couldn't face the pain of loss? He couldn't believe God had anything to do with that. Or that his father ever considered how his absence had hurt his son and his mother.

But sharing his thoughts about his dad would only cause Nonna more pain. A good reason to keep those thoughts to himself from here on out. Just like Maggie had advised him. Add wise to her list of attributes. But didn't he have more to say? Wasn't it past time to do what he'd come back to do? "I'm sorry, Nonna."

Nonna gave him a questioning look. "Sorry?"

He made himself meet her gaze. "For giving you… you know, a rough time growing up."

"Oh, my dear Anthony." She patted his hand. "You were young, everything black-and-white, no grays. It was very hard for you without your father. And perhaps I was too strict at times." She smiled. "You were such a handsome boy, deeply passionate…and headstrong, too…much like my Salvatore."

She'd elevated him enough to compare him to his grandfather?

She carefully turned pages. "As for your father, there

is a picture of you with your mamma and papa. You will
see the love he had for you."

Oh, boy. He hoped she didn't mean the picture—

She scowled up at him as she pointed to the blank
spot. "Where is the photo?"

The one of him on his father's shoulders. The one
he'd yanked from the album and left in the trunk. Why,
he didn't know. And he didn't have a clue how to explain to her what he couldn't understand himself.

"It is a precious picture, Anthony. You must find it
and put it back in the album where it belongs."

The last thing he wanted to do was upset her. He
stood up, chair legs screeching against the tile floor.

Nonna gave him a startled look. "Do not run away,
Anthony."

Run away? "I'm not running away, Nonna." He
grabbed the stack of albums. "I'm going to find that
picture for you. I'm sure it's in the trunk."

He strode out of the room and down the hall. Why
had he taken that picture out of the album? He didn't
know why. He only knew he felt too much when he
looked at it.

And he hadn't wanted to go there with Nonna.

Della's place was humming, the buzz of conversa-
tions and clatter of dishes deafening. Tony sat across
from Maggie in a back booth waiting for Hannah to
bring their suppers. Maggie had asked him to meet her.
Actually, it had bordered more on a command than a re-
quest. She must be having a bad day. "You saw Nonna?"

"I tried, but she was asleep at 4:00 p.m."

"I took lunch to her," he said. "She actually seemed
to enjoy it, and we looked at one of the old photo albums
I took from the attic."

"Really?" Rather than looking pleased, she frowned at him suspiciously.

His defense mechanism began clicking in, and he wasn't sure what he'd done to deserve suspicion. "The picture album was such a hit, she wouldn't hear of taking a nap until we looked at another one."

Maggie drew in a breath and let it out a little too carefully. "Jim said she's developed a cold and is running a low-grade fever."

"You think I tired her out too much?"

"I don't think you made her sick, if that's what you mean. But Jim said she's fretting about a lost picture and worried you'll leave without telling her. What happened, Tony?"

He pressed his hand to his forehead, trying to think his way through an unexpected quagmire. Maggie hadn't come out and accused him of upsetting his nonna, but she didn't have to. He got the picture.

"What happened?" Her voice shook. With worry? Agitation? Or restraint?

"We had a good time. We talked a little about my growing-up years, she helped me understand my dad a little—"

"Your dad?" Maggie gave him a look that clearly questioned his sanity.

He lifted a hand to slow her down. "I know what you're thinking…but it was good…good enough that I managed to ask her to forgive me, and she did. In fact, if she hadn't looked for the picture to show me, she might not have even noticed it was missing."

"What picture?" Maggie frowned.

He looked down at the table. "The one we saw in the attic."

"Of you and your parents?"

He nodded. "I took it out, for some reason. Do you think she was more upset about that picture than I thought?"

"Did you mention going back to South America?"

He shook his head. "Neither of us did. I specifically told her I was going to find the picture. I don't remember telling her I'd see her tomorrow. I should have told her that, shouldn't I?"

"You need to make it clear you'll tell her before you leave."

"I will." God knew Maggie understood the torture of loved ones being gone without her having the chance to tell them goodbye.

"Dr. Peterson doesn't want her doing therapy for a few days until her cold clears up." Tears glistened in her eyes. "She's going to be so discouraged. And with you leaving…I don't know what I'm going to do to keep her from giving up."

"She's a fighter, Maggie. She's not going to give up. You have to believe that."

She took a sip of water. "I do…when I remember to put everything in God's hands and leave it there."

"Not an easy thing to remember sometimes." He dragged a breath and decided a change of topic might help. "Too bad they're out of your favorite custard pie again. I'd like to see if it lives up to your endorsement." He realized unless he came here for breakfast tomorrow, this would be the last time he ate here for a good long time. "I'll cook tomorrow night, okay?"

"Okay. Tomorrow will be your last night before you go back to your jungle."

"Yeah." He swallowed, hating the thought of leaving Maggie. Especially when he still hadn't found a way to get past her logic glitch about the old house.

"How's Stella?" Della hustled by, a steaming plate of food in each hand.

Maggie shook her head.

"I'll be right back." Looking concerned, Della delivered the food to two teenage girls wearing Noah's Crossing softball shirts and caps.

Tony gave Maggie a serious look. "Whatever you tell Della will be broadcast all over town. You do know that, right?"

"That's the idea. We depend on her to know what's going on in town and to keep us informed."

Tony grunted as if he understood. He didn't.

"Stella isn't doing so well?" Della was back, apprehension in her voice.

"She has a cold and can't do her therapy," Maggie explained anxiously.

"That doesn't sound good."

"No. We need to do everything we can think of to keep her from getting discouraged."

"People are sending cards. I've told them that you said she needs rest and therapy right now. But maybe a few of her friends could stop in to help cheer her up. What do you think?"

"I don't know." Maggie frowned.

"She needs time to recover," Tony said simply. "Seeing people will tire her out."

Maggie nodded. "But she used to see her friends when she did errands or met with her church groups. I'm sure she misses them."

"There's nothing like a familiar face and a warm hug," Della said.

"Hmm," Maggie murmured. "Maybe if somebody stopped in for five or ten minutes in the morning and afternoon. That would give her plenty of time for rest."

"I'll be happy to talk to Jim about timing and keep a schedule here for people to sign up," Della offered.

"That's very generous," Maggie said.

The bell by the cash register pinged, alerting Della that a customer was waiting to pay for food. "You two think about it." Della hustled away.

"I'm sure Stella would love to see her friends," Maggie said.

He wasn't convinced.

"When either of us is there, she seems to perk up. But obviously, we can't be there all the time. And when you leave…well, we know she won't take that well."

Hannah set plates of roast beef, potatoes and steamed vegetables in front of them.

"Thanks, Hannah," he said.

Hannah's chubby face lit in a smile. "If you need anything else, let me know." She walked away, more confidence in her demeanor than he remembered. Good for Hannah.

He cut a slice of beef, took a bite, added pepper. "Do you really think her friends would stick to a schedule and stay only five or ten minutes?"

"We'll tell Della to stress how important it is that they not tire her."

"You have more faith in people than I do."

"I'll ask the aide to keep her eye on the clock when people visit. But these people are her friends, Tony. They have her best interest at heart."

He guessed that's what friends did, didn't they? "But I think we'd better run the idea by her doctor first. If he gives it a thumbs-up, let's give it a try."

"Good." She picked at her food as if she didn't have much of an appetite.

Tony took a drink of his soda, set down the glass and

decided to wade in and find out just how bad her day had been. "How did your meeting go?"

"Not so good."

"What's wrong with those people? They, obviously, don't know good landscaping."

Her gaze darted nervously to the table.

Was she hiding something? "The meeting wasn't with a potential client?"

"It was with a loan officer."

He squinted. "Please tell me you didn't ask him for a loan to fix Nonna's house."

She gave him a guilty frown and set out to explain an elaborate scheme to use the potential of a rose as collateral for a loan.

He'd never heard anything so ridiculously speculative in his life. "Did you get the loan?" he asked as calmly as he could.

"No." She lifted her chin. "I guess I might just as well tell you all the bad news while I'm at it. I've called several banks in Eau Claire, too. They're not interested in loaning me money either."

He gave her the most sympathetic look he could muster. "When are you going to stop beating your head against a rock?"

She met his gaze and held it. "You're absolutely no help when you ask a question like that."

"Help?" He gave her a narrow-eyed look. "You've flatly turned down my offers of help."

She huffed and shoveled in a huge bite of food, as if her appetite had suddenly picked up.

Too bad he'd lost his. He had one day left to convince her the old house was a total wash. One day. Not too likely when he'd already given her his best arguments and wasn't coming up with any new ones. Maybe he should get a clue that she wasn't listening to him.

Wait just a minute. She wasn't listening to *him*. That didn't mean she wouldn't listen to somebody else… necessarily. Especially if that somebody was an expert on old houses.

Like Jack Celenti.

The last Tony heard, Jack had slunk off to Minneapolis last year to nurse a bad case of malaria. Minneapolis was practically in their backyard…relatively speaking. "Are you free tomorrow afternoon?"

"I have a meeting with Senator Benson's wife at three, which reminds me, I need to get home and finish the plans I'm drawing for her. But I should be free by four or so. Why?"

"I know a guy who loves old houses and knows them like the back of his hand. I think he's currently living in Minneapolis. I'll give him a call, see if he can drive over tomorrow for a quick reunion and a house assessment."

She studied him, her fork poised halfway to her mouth. "You'd do that?"

"Unless you're ready to change your mind about the house?" He raised an eyebrow.

She gave him a serious stare.

He sighed resignedly. "Well, then…I'll give the expert a call."

Chapter Ten

"It's nice to see you again, Ms. McGuire." Senator Benson's wife swept into the sunroom like a regal delphinium, tall and flouncy and all in bright blue. "I'm very excited to look at the plans you've drawn for my rose garden."

Smiling in greeting, Maggie shook the woman's offered hand and held out the roses she brought for the senator's wife.

"What exquisite roses. The coral-pink color is so unusual." Mrs. Benson took a deep breath. "And the fragrance is lovely."

The Salvatore roses were weaving their charms just as Maggie hoped they would. "They're my gift to you. I thought you might enjoy them."

"I certainly will. As you know, roses are one of my passions. Please, sit down." Mrs. Benson sat. "Thank you so much for the roses."

"You're very welcome." Doing her best to calm her racing mind, Maggie laid her sketchbook and notepad on the glass-top table, perched on one of the cushioned chairs and began spreading out her designs for easy viewing.

She hoped Mrs. Benson also loved the rose garden drawings that she'd stayed up half the night to finish. But whether the lady loved the roses or the sketches wasn't what had her so on edge.

It was obvious bank loan officers weren't lining up to give her a loan based on future earnings of the rose. But on the way to Rainbow Lake, the wonderful scent of the Salvatore roses filling her truck had given her a lightbulb idea.

What about a private backer?

Mrs. Benson seemed made to order, and this appointment gave Maggie an opportunity she couldn't pass up. Not only did the senator's wife adore roses, but she also seemed wealthy enough to wait for the investment to pay off. If Maggie signed over future rights to profits, she could claim a salary above and beyond the costs for propagating the rose. And voilà. No more cash flow problems. No more trouble getting a loan or paying it off.

She'd have to be extremely tactful in her timing and choice of words when she presented her need for a financial backer. She didn't relish the possibility of embarrassing herself. Or even worse, Mrs. Benson. "As you can see, I've done three sketches of possible layouts for the rose garden, incorporating ideas we talked about."

Mrs. Benson donned the glasses hanging from a gold chain around her neck and peered at the first sketch. "Very nice."

"I've attempted to convey a different shape and flow in each design, but any of the elements you like can be worked into the final plan."

While Mrs. Benson took her time to study each sketch, Maggie nibbled discreetly on a fingernail and tried to calm her mind for her little spiel about the Salvatore rose.

Finally, Mrs. Benson pushed her glasses higher on her nose. "You've captured the ambience I love in all three of your designs, but I believe I prefer the second one. I like the way the trellises and arbors draw the eye up. I also like the flagstone walk, the benches and the quaint little fountain you show in the other drawings."

"All those elements will work together beautifully." Maggie made notes, appreciating Mrs. Benson's eye for detail. Many of her clients hardly glanced at her carefully laid-out designs, preferring not to be bothered with the particulars.

"I see you have identified the roses by name, color, bloom time and intensity of fragrance. But I don't see this lovely coral-pink rose you brought me today." Mrs. Benson peered over her glasses at Maggie. "It is an exceptional one. I want it planted near the benches to allow guests to enjoy its fragrance."

Maggie had trouble containing her smile. Mrs. Benson *had* fallen in love with the Salvatore rose. Whether she'd be interested enough to become a financial backer for its propagation was the question. A question Maggie had to find just the proper way to phrase. "It's a magnificent rose, but it hasn't been propagated for commercial use."

Mrs. Benson frowned in puzzlement. "I hope it isn't too delicate for this climate. The roses are so fresh, I assumed you'd just cut them."

"The rose was bred for northern Wisconsin's climate. And yes, I cut them just before I brought them to you."

"I don't understand."

Careful, she told herself. She couldn't afford to gush or appear too excited and blow her professional image.

"The Salvatore rose grows exclusively in a private garden near Noah's Crossing."

Mrs. Benson shook her head. "What a shame. It's a wonderful rose. What a rare gift. Thank you again."

Maggie smiled. Rather, she beamed. She'd never have a better opening. "A good friend and her late husband bred the rose years ago. I recently talked to her about my developing it. She's very interested, but we need a financial backer to make it happen."

Mrs. Benson's eyes widened in a look of surprise. "I see."

Maggie almost cringed. Had she offended the lady by stating her need so succinctly?

"I'd be very disappointed if I couldn't have that rose in my garden."

Just as she'd hoped Mrs. Benson would feel. "This season, I could plant an inexpensive rose near the benches, anticipating the availability of the Salvatore rose in the future."

"There's no chance it will be available this summer?"

"I could get one or two plants. But it will take a season to propagate more. And I'm afraid I can't do that without a backer."

A tiny frown creased Mrs. Benson's forehead. "I'd be very interested in backing you myself. Unfortunately, I've taken on my quota of projects for the next couple years. I would like you to reserve spots in the garden for the rose in case you find a backer, though."

"I…I…understand." She struggled to keep her expression from showing her disappointment. "I'll draw up a plan incorporating your preferences and call to schedule another meeting for your final approval."

"I'll wait to hear from you." Mrs. Benson stood.

Maggie got up, gathered her sketch pad and notebook

into her portfolio. Hands shaking, she tried to steady them, not wanting Mrs. Benson to notice. She'd have to find another rose enthusiast to fund the rose.

If only she knew of one.

Sun blazing across the western sky in an orange-streaked sunset, Tony and his old friend Jack Celenti sat on the back steps drinking lemonade and catching up on news. Tony's head jerked up when tires crunched gravel.

Maggie's Suburban pulled to a stop in the driveway. She slammed the door shut, and walked toward them, confident, self-possessed, irresistible.

Both men climbed to their feet.

She stopped in front of them.

"Maggie, this is Jack Celenti. Jack, Maggie McGuire."

"It's a real pleasure to meet you, Ms. McGuire." Jack grabbed Maggie's small hand and pumped it with vigor. "How come you didn't tell me she was such a beauty, Stefano?"

Tony drew in a long breath. Jack's fancy for women usually amused Tony, but Maggie could be put off by him.

Her lips turned up in a tired little smile but her assessing brown eyes never flickered. "It's nice to meet one of Tony's friends, Mr. Celenti."

"The pleasure is mine, little lady, believe me." Jack grinned.

"Subtlety escapes him, but Jack's a genius when it comes to old houses," Tony said.

"At your service." Jack did a flamboyant bow.

Tony couldn't help chuckling. What a ham.

Maggie set her oversize briefcase on the bottom step, her shoulders drooping a little.

"Rough day?" Tony asked.

"You might say that."

"Mrs. Benson didn't love those great designs of yours?"

"She liked them." A little frown clouded her eyes. "I stopped to see Stella on the way home. She's not doing so well, but Dr. Peterson thinks short visits with friends could help her state of mind."

She sounded exhausted. The last thing she needed right now was Jack's analysis of the house. But Tony couldn't put it off. Not when he was flying out tomorrow. She and Nonna needed a place to live that wasn't falling down and too expensive to fix. Hopefully, a little dose of reality would convince Maggie of that. "I stopped to see Nonna this morning," he said. No need to mention that Nonna barely woke up to greet him.

Maggie's shoulders bunched as the word *Nonna* left his lips. "Let's get started."

Tony wished she'd relax a little. This inspection didn't have to be a nail-biting venture. "Can I get you some lemonade?"

"No, thank you. I'm very anxious to hear what Mr. Celenti has to say."

"To begin with, the presentation of the Victorian is magnificent. There are no flaws in the setting or the layout. I recommend nothing be changed in that category."

Leave it to Jack to play up the strengths first. But Maggie would see right through his telling her what she wanted to hear.

Jack walked over and parted the plants near the foundation. He inspected the rock wall and soon disappeared around the corner of the house.

Maggie took off as if she dared not let him out of her sight.

Careful not to damage the plantings, Jack continued along the circumference of the house with Maggie on his heels. Tony followed. Occasionally, the expert rubbed his large hand over the dry, peeling paint, flakes shimmering down to drift over plants and flowers like snow. From time to time, he inspected a rotting windowsill.

"Well?" Maggie said sharply, obviously unable to endure Jack's silence any longer. "Can you give us your thoughts, Mr. Celenti?"

Jack took a red kerchief from his hip pocket and mopped his face. "Please call me Jack. I'll check the foundation in the cellar later. But from the outside, it appears it was built to last."

Maggie gave Tony a little smile of satisfaction. Apparently, she figured a good foundation was all the place needed.

"The siding has seen better days," Jack went on. "It needs to be ripped off and replaced with new before it's painted. And the house should be wrapped with insulation to keep these horrific winter winds out." Jack gave Tony a pained look. "I'll never get used to these northern winters."

Tony nodded, even though he hadn't lived through a northern winter for a good long time.

"Every last window needs to be replaced, which will increase energy efficiency. You'll have to decide if you want to change the openings to accommodate regular windows or have windows built to fit. Now, I'll use that ladder to inspect the roof."

Maggie wore her worried look. The one that made Tony want to comfort her. She was probably watching dollar signs dance before her eyes. And now, Jack was heading to the roof. She already knew the sorry state of that part of the house.

Tony hated putting her through this, but she had to know what she would be up against if she took on the old place. He adjusted the ladder and held it.

Jack began to climb. "You two stay down here. That's a real steep pitch and the shingles are probably moss-covered and slippery."

"Be careful. You could fall through," Tony warned.

Jack hauled himself onto the roof with the nimbleness that always amazed Tony. A minute later, the expert disappeared from sight.

Maggie kept on gazing up. "Have you known Jack long?"

"About six years. He's a good guy and a hard worker."

"He says the foundation is good. That's the most important thing." She set her chin as if she had all the corroboration she needed to sink tons of money into the old house.

"Do you have any idea the cost of the things he mentioned? Plus we know what shape the roof is in. And he hasn't even gotten to the interior."

She shook her head, as if none of it mattered. "I'm willing to listen to your objective expert's opinion. Shouldn't you be just as willing? Unless you've already told Jack what his opinion should be."

Tony couldn't believe his ears. "Come on, you don't think I got Jack over here to lie to you."

"I know you're convinced the house isn't worth saving."

"Who do you think I am, Maggie? A liar?"

She gave her head a little shake. "I'm sorry. I know you wouldn't lie to me. It's just…" She drew in a breath, let it out. "I'm sorry."

He ignored the impulse to take her hand in his and rubbed the back of his neck instead. What was he getting in such a snit about? You'd think she'd accused him of murder. Although if she had, it probably wouldn't hurt more.

"Hey, Stefano. Steady that ladder so I can get on it without killing myself, will you?"

Relieved by the interruption, Tony grasped the ladder firmly.

Once Jack reached the ground, he paced a few steps toward the porch, then turned and paced back, shaking his head and puffing on his cigar. He stopped in front of Maggie, looking as sorrowful as Tony had ever seen him. "Well, both chimneys are beyond repair. And the roof is a total loss. It will have to be built from scratch."

Jack was a man who dealt with practicalities and financial bottom lines. The least he could do was attach a price tag to his ideas. "We need to know how much things will cost, Jack."

Tony didn't add, because neither she nor Nonna have the money to restore a cottage, let alone a monstrous place like this one. "The beams in the attic are rotting, too. How much money are we talking?"

Jack rubbed his head. "Rebuilding the entire top of the house with the gables and dormers, I'd say we're talking in the neighborhood of fifty thousand dollars for materials and labor.

"Wow, those estimates are even steeper than I thought," Tony said.

Jack met Maggie's eyes, his usually jovial expression grave. "The roof is the first priority. It's in terrible shape. Rewiring should be addressed next. The wiring is always brittle in these old houses, and there's not much point in sinking money in a tinderbox."

"What neighborhood are we talking for the rewiring?" Tony couldn't help feeling like a Judas for asking, but it had to be done if Maggie was going to get the complete picture.

Jack gave his cigar a couple puffs and launched into a list of costs that mounted well beyond Tony's rough calculation.

Maggie bit her lip. The fight seemed to be draining out of her before his eyes. She'd had her heart so set on having the old place ready for Nonna to come back home to live.

He hated this. Hurting her was the last thing he wanted to do. "She's heard enough, Jack."

"No, I want to know what needs to be done. What else, Mr. Celenti...Jack?"

Jack glanced at Tony, then focused on Maggie again. "I'll need to take a look inside."

Tony grimaced. Maggie was as pale as a ghost, her body so rigid that she looked as though she might launch into space any minute. Time to end this session. "I think you've seen enough to get to the bottom line, Jack. If this place was yours, what would you do?"

Jack cleared his throat as if to lend drama to his pronouncement. "I love old houses, so it pains me to say this. But considering the financial outlay needed to restore this one, I'd advise tearing it down and building from the foundation up."

Maggie flinched as though she'd been hit. Her lovely face began to crumple as she fought for composure.

Tony reached out to her. He needed to comfort her.

"It's Stella's home." She twisted away, staring at him through eyes filled with hurt. "We can't tear it down."

His heart thudded so hard, he could scarcely breathe. Whatever made him think calling Jack was a good idea? "Maggie—"

"We can't." She flung the words at him, then she turned and ran up the front steps and disappeared behind the roses climbing the porch. The door slammed with a resounding bang.

Tony raced inside. Maggie never ran away from anything. Never.

Chapter Eleven

Gut churning, Tony gave two raps on Maggie's bedroom door. "It's me."

Silence. She didn't throw a shoe at the door. She didn't tell him to go away. She ignored him. She probably wanted to be alone to compose herself, but he needed to make sure she was all right. Somehow, he needed to erase that look he'd seen in her eyes, the look he'd never seen there before. Fear and lost hope.

Guilt twisting inside him, he turned the ancient knob and pushed open the door.

At first he didn't see her. Then he spotted the top of her head near the window on the other side of the high four-poster. He walked around the bed and lowered himself to his haunches beside her. "You okay?"

She shook her head.

He began to reach out to touch her face, then decided against it. His touch was probably the last thing she'd welcome right now.

She just sat there, hugging her knees and staring out the darkening window. She looked so forlorn. So crushed.

If only she'd cry or holler at him or throw things,

he might be able to think of something to say or do. As it was, he had nothing to take his mind off the pain spreading through him. "I'm sorry, Maggie."

"For what?" Although there was an edge in her voice, she didn't move or turn to him. She just kept staring out that window.

"I'm sorry the house isn't in better shape. That there's not much money to repair it. Mostly, I'm sorry I didn't see how much Jack's evaluation would upset you."

"That's sweet."

He dragged a heavy breath. He wanted to grasp her shoulders and turn her to face him, but he resisted the impulse. "Talk to me, Maggie."

"I've talked far too much."

"No, you haven't."

"You don't hear me."

He couldn't believe his ears. He'd heard her every word. "When? When haven't I heard you?"

She jerked around to face him, her eyes dark and accusing. "You think I'm being stubborn about Stella's house. You think I'm daydreaming about fixing it up. Why can't you understand?" She waved her hands wildly with each word. "Stella *needs* her home. Don't you care about that?"

"Of course I care." He felt sick to his stomach seeing her hurting like this. "Calm down, okay?"

She gave him a look of disgust and threw her hands in the air. "Make up your mind. You told me to talk to you. But I can't talk and calm down at the same time."

He rubbed the back of his neck to ease the tension. "Don't you think I'd like Nonna to be able to return to her home?"

She glared at him, murder in her eyes. Then she

turned abruptly and stared out the window again. "I had no idea how much it would cost, but we can't tear down Stella's house. Not being able to come home will...kill...her."

Tony's insides turned inside out. Oh, yeah, fine thing he'd done by inviting Jack. Maggie was absolutely beaten, and he didn't have a clue what to say to help her out. Probably best to keep his mouth shut. The last thing he wanted was to say the wrong thing. But he had to do something. Carefully, he laid his hand on her shoulder.

She stiffened.

Aching with the need to make things better, it was all he could do to keep from gathering her in his arms and promising her the moon if only she'd act like herself again.

Too bad he didn't have the moon to give her. And if he tried to take her in his arms, she'd probably order him out of her room. So he gently stroked her shoulder while his stomach churned like a cement mixer.

One thing was clear. He couldn't let her go on struggling alone. Sure, she was self-sufficient and capable, but she needed help and there was one thing he could help her with. "Maggie, we won't tear Nonna's house down."

She turned to look at him, her brow puckering in a puzzled frown. "You're just saying that to make me feel better."

"I promise."

"But the money..."

He smoothed her curls back and tilted her head so she had to look at him. "Those checks in the cookie jar will pay for materials for the roof."

"Stella refused to let me use them."

Of course she did. "I'll talk to her."

She worried her bottom lip, doubt in her eyes. "But that's not—"

"Do you trust me?"

Still frowning, she gave a little nod.

He let out a breath he hadn't realized he was holding. She trusted him. Now all he needed was to figure out what he was going to do. If he'd stashed away the big bucks he'd made over the years rather than buying materials to build schools in the strife-torn areas he'd worked in, the answer would be simple.

The money he'd sent to Nonna and the savings he'd put away for a rainy day were a start. But the money wouldn't stretch far enough to pay for materials *and* labor. So what was he going to do? He didn't know. But whatever he came up with, he was going to help Maggie. Running out on her was not an option.

Not this time.

Early Friday morning, Maggie pulled into the driveway alongside Tony's motorcycle. She'd gone to the rehab center early to check on Stella with her own eyes. Her friend's fever was down a degree. *Thank You, God, but she still looks so pale and weak. Please help her. And please help her deal with Tony leaving today.*

He was probably packed up, ready to ride out of her life. Who knew when or if she'd ever see him again? Tears threatening, she did her best to will them away. *Thank You for giving me the chance to tell him goodbye. Please help me find the words.* She jumped out of the Suburban, grabbed her portfolio from the seat and slammed the door.

Loud crashes came from the top of the house. Alarm

jolted her. Peering up, she couldn't see the source of the noise. What in the world was going on?

Another loud crash made her jump. It sounded as if somebody was tearing down the house. Had Tony hired a carpenter? She raced up the back steps and through the door. She dropped her portfolio on a nearby chair, bolted through the kitchen and up the stairs. Breathlessly, she reached the attic door and pulled it open. A tearing sound and another crash assaulted her. She charged up the narrow stairs, choking on dust and hot air.

Reaching the attic, she squinted through the haze. The first thing she saw was the sky. Part of the roof was gone. It lay in a heap of rubble on the attic floor. And in the middle of the debris, shirtless and grabbing at the ceiling with a crowbar, stood Tony. Confusion and panic flared inside her. "Tony," she yelled.

He jerked around to face her, his eyes wide with surprise, his face and chest streaked with sweat and grime.

He looked so strong. So powerful. She stared, trying to catch her breath, unable to focus on anything but him.

His eyes shone with intent. His muscles glistened with the sheen of hard labor. He stood tall with the pride of earnest sweat. He was clearly in his element, working with his hands and totally in charge. A grin began in his eyes and spread over his face. "Don't worry, Blossom. I moved the old trunk and stuff to one of the spare bedrooms."

"But you promised *not* to tear down the house." Without waiting for his reply, she climbed the pile of rubble, her sandals slipping and stumbling until she stood in front of him.

He lowered the crowbar. "I'm tearing out the rotted wood so I can rebuild."

"But there's nothing to keep out the rain." She pointed helplessly at the expanse of sky where the roof should have been.

He shot her a teasing grin. "There was nothing to keep out the rain before either. But not to worry, I'll rig up a plastic tent."

"You…you have to catch your flight."

"I canceled."

"Canceled?"

"I'm staying to do the labor myself."

"Staying?"

"I told you I'd help."

She shook her head. He was *staying?* But he hadn't said he was staying last night. She would remember if he'd said he was staying. "You said the money in the cookie jar would pay for materials for the roof."

"It will. And I have a small nest egg stashed away, too. It's not nearly enough, but the money will go a lot further if I do the labor."

"What about your project in Brazil?"

"I have a good foreman on-site, a guy who's been with me awhile and knows how I run things. And I'm working on getting better communications in place so I can help him deal with problems more efficiently and keep my backers happy."

She shook her head, still trying to sort things out. "You can do that? Did your backers agree? Will you get in trouble? Why are you doing this?"

He squinted. "Yes, yes, no and, most important, I can't leave when Nonna needs me." He shifted his focus to a spot beyond her shoulder. "When *you* need me."

Could he be saying what she thought he was saying?

Could he actually be the Tony she'd dreamed about all these years? A smile spread until it consumed her. Stepping closer, she reached out and grasped his hand.

He dropped the crowbar with a thud. His gaze dark, intense, he questioned her with his eyes.

"You're really staying?"

He smiled that Tony smile. "I'm really staying."

But for how long? a small voice in the back of her mind nudged. "How long?"

"Am I staying?"

She managed a nod.

"Long enough to get the roof and bathroom ready for Nonna to come home. At least a couple months."

She shivered. "A couple months," she whispered.

"Give or take." His eyes flinched. "You thought…"

She'd hoped.

He blew out a breath. "I wish I could promise to stay longer. But…"

She knew he couldn't. Deep down she knew, but that didn't make it any easier. No man but Tony had ever made her feel like she'd rather be with him than anyplace else on earth. She doubted any other man ever would.

Tony spent the next day ripping the roof apart, too agitated even to visit Nonna. How could he focus on safe pleasantries when he was sleep-deprived and so mixed-up about Maggie? Knee-deep in rubble and running out of daylight, he flexed his tired shoulder muscles and surveyed his demolition progress. At least he had something to vent his confusion on.

Roaring through the countryside on the bike last night hadn't helped one bit to straighten out his mind. Tearing the roof apart today wasn't helping either. Not with the memory of the joy in Maggie's eyes when he told her he was staying. Nor the plea in her voice when she'd asked him how long.

He'd wanted to promise her forever, but he cared about her too much to make a promise he couldn't keep. He stomped down the attic steps to take a shower and start supper.

An hour later, he ground more pepper into the sauce simmering on the stove and tried to ignore the clock on the wall. Nonna would be sacked out by now, so Maggie couldn't still be at the rehab center.

He grabbed a bottle of soda from the refrigerator and went out to sit on the back step. Stars glittered in the black sky like diamonds, fireflies blinked in the still night and frogs sang their mournful melodies.

Where was she?

A car pulling into the driveway had him on his feet when he realized it was Hannah's brother dropping her off after she'd spent the day celebrating a family birthday near Eau Claire. Maybe she knew where Maggie was.

The car took off and Hannah bustled up the walk like she had something important on her mind. She gave him a nervous smile.

"Did you have a good time with your family?" he asked.

Nodding, she frowned up at him. "Maggie's car isn't here. Do you know where she is?"

"No clue. She didn't mention she had plans tonight?" Hannah shook her head.

Another car pulled into the driveway. A car, not the Suburban. Suddenly, this place was a hub of activity.

"Uh…that's Lucas," Hannah said. "He invited me to watch a movie at his gram's house. Do you think it will be okay with Maggie if I stay out a little later than eleven? I'll still be up early for church, okay?"

Tony squinted. Apparently, Hannah knew Maggie took her responsibility for her young charge seriously. But Maggie wasn't here, was she? So he had to wing it. "How about being home by midnight?"

"Thank you." Smiling brightly, Hannah hurried to the car.

Lucas held the passenger door open for her.

She got in.

Lucas gave Tony a wave, got in behind the wheel and drove off.

Tony went back to studying the stars. He just couldn't shake the feeling Maggie was in trouble. Absurd. She'd been taking care of herself for years. Besides, he wasn't a guy who worried.

But what if that ancient Suburban finally gave up the ghost? He raked his hand through his hair. If she was in trouble, she'd use her cell to call him for help, wouldn't she? Of course she would.

In fact, he could call her right now to make sure she was all right. *If* he had her cell number.

He glared at a firefly until it disappeared into the woods. Then he got up and went into the house to stir the sauce, his gaze wandering to the old clock. Ten o'clock.

What if she'd called while he was pounding in the attic or taking a shower? Too bad Nonna didn't have voice mail or an answering machine at the house.

He had to do something. He headed for the door, then turned and took the stairs two at a time, grabbed his wallet and keys from the bureau and charged back down the steps and out the door.

He jumped onto the Harley, jammed his helmet

and visor in place and spit gravel as he peeled out of the driveway. Roaring past Maggie's greenhouse, he scanned the parking lot for her Suburban. The lot was empty, the place dark and deserted.

Maybe she'd made plans with friends. That was probably it. He considered turning back. But his imagination tortured him with visions of her walking beside the dark road. Or unconscious behind the steering wheel after a hit-and-run accident. He pushed the thoughts away and leaned into the turn.

Sweeping the roadside with his gaze, he tried to ignore the anxiety gnawing in his belly. He eased up on the throttle to take a curve as he met an oncoming car. Then he caught a glimpse of Maggie's truck parked on the opposite side of the road, its headlights shining on a little, beat-up blue pickup parked on the shoulder in front of it.

He slammed on his brakes and skidded through a U-turn in the middle of the road. He pulled off the asphalt and braked to a stop beside Maggie's truck, searching for any sign of her in the glare of her headlights.

He spotted her on her knees near the right front fender of the jacked-up pickup. Killing the motor, he climbed off the bike.

Eyes wide, she ran to him, a spray can in her hand. "Did something happen with Stella?" she asked in alarm.

"She's fine."

"Then what are you doing here?"

He did his best to think of an answer, not easy with a profound sense of relief overriding the confusion and worry muddling his mind. Fighting the urge to haul her into his arms, he whipped off his helmet. "Uh…I ran out of soda." Actually true.

The tailgate door on her Suburban slammed shut. A teenage boy in baggy jeans and a small gold ring glittering in his nose strode to Maggie, holding a lug wrench out to her. "Is this the wrench you meant?"

"That's the one."

No flimsy tire iron for Maggie. Leave it to her to have the heavy-duty, four-way lug wrench that always got the job done.

Maggie gestured an introduction. "Tony…Eric."

"Hi." The kid held up a hand.

Tony frowned. "Having trouble with your truck?"

"Just a flat. But the lug nuts are so rusted, I can't get them off."

"WD-40 to the rescue." Maggie sank to her knees by the tire and sprayed the lug nuts like a pro.

Tony blew out a breath and stared at her. "Why don't you use your cell phone for emergencies?"

"We don't have an emergency, do we, Eric?"

Tony shook his head. "What would constitute an emergency?"

"A lot more than a flat tire and rusty lug nuts." She gave him an amused look.

He wasn't feeling amused. "Well, you could use your cell to let people know you're not lying dead along the highway."

She stared up at him wide-eyed. "What people?"

He clenched his jaw.

Understanding dawned in her brown eyes. "*You* thought I was lying dead along the highway?"

"You're very late."

At least, she looked a little contrite. "I had no idea you'd worry."

He was pretty surprised himself. "I wasn't worried." He rubbed the back of his neck. "Hannah wanted to ask your permission to stay out past eleven."

"Why?"

"To watch a movie with Lucas at his grandmother's place. I told her she could stay out until twelve."

Maggie frowned. "Did you call Lucas's grandmother to verify?"

"Never gave it a thought. Hannah's trustworthy, isn't she?"

"Usually. But we don't know Lucas, and he is several years older than she is."

"It would have helped to know how to reach you."

"Hannah has my cell number." She gave him a knowing look. "Apparently, our little Hannah thought you'd be more lenient. Turns out, she was right."

Had Hannah set him up? She'd at least misled him. But what did he know about teenage girls? He *did* know enough about teenage boys to be a little worried. Too bad he hadn't thought about that earlier. He sure seemed to be doing a lot of worrying lately…for a guy who didn't worry. "Where have you been?"

She set the can of WD-40 on the ground beside her, reached to take the lug wrench from Eric and looked up at Tony. "Let's see. I worked all day, then stopped to see Stella. She's happy you're staying for a while, but said she hadn't seen you today. She's feeling a little better and seemed happy one of her friends had visited for a few minutes."

He kicked gravel. "Nonna went to sleep hours ago."

Maggie studied him. "This evening, I helped Dixie Rodar throw a baby shower for Rachel. Well, Dixie Carpenter now. She married Jeff."

He stared blankly, too absorbed in the sound of her voice to have a clue who she was talking about.

"You remember. Dixie and Jessie and I were best friends all through school. We used to have so much fun." She gave him a sad look. "Now Jessie's married and living in Madison. And Dixie and I are both so busy, we hardly see each other anymore."

She sure didn't like changes in her life. He shrugged off a pang of worry. Enough with the worry. "Life moves on, Maggie," he said gently.

She nodded. "I'm getting the picture."

Twirling his helmet in his hands, he figured maybe she wasn't talking about her and Dixie anymore.

She fit the wrench to a lug nut and gave it a mighty yank. Her biceps bunched, her neck muscles strained and the tip of her tongue peeked from between her lips. She thought she could get that tire off with a squirt of WD-40 and sheer willpower. But what else was new?

The lug nut began to turn.

"It's working," the kid yelled. "I can take it from here, Maggie."

"Be my guest." She stood and let the boy take her place.

No doubt, the poor kid was trying to save face. It could be hard when a guy had to depend on a girl to help him change a tire. And it was pretty obvious that girl had everything under control. She didn't need Tony's help as usual. "I guess I'll head back before that delicious sauce loses its freshness." He turned and strolled toward the beam of his headlights.

"Hey, save some for me," she called.

He liked that familiar feisty tone. It told him things between them might be getting back to normal. Well, as normal as they could be after he'd wiped that beautiful smile off her face yesterday.

Is that what he wanted with Maggie? Normalcy?

Not by a long shot. He wanted her to need him. He wanted her trust. He wanted her faith in God, her positive outlook and her passion for life. And he wanted every bit of her attention focused on him.

Which was never going to happen. Not when he'd be leaving in a couple of months. But she was all right. That had to be enough.

Chapter Twelve

Maggie marched from the door to the kitchen window. "Still no sign of headlights turning into the driveway. Where is she?"

"If you don't stop pacing, you're going to wear out the floor," Tony said helpfully.

Shooting him an irritated glance, she interrupted her latest trek across the kitchen. Her gaze darted to the old clock on its shelf over the sink. One-ten.

"It's exactly two minutes since you last checked," Tony said dolefully. "Why don't you sit down like a sane person, and we'll go over sensible reasons Hannah could be late?"

Whirling, she stomped over to the table and perched on a chair opposite him. "Sensible reasons like what?"

"Let's see if we can figure out a few. Lucas picked up Hannah about nine-thirty."

Maggie pressed her hand to her forehead. "Over *three and a half* hours ago."

"Lucas' grandmother said they were going to the movie at Dun Harbor." Tony pointed at the *Noah's Crossing Courier* on the table in front of him. "The movie didn't start until ten-twenty, probably lasted close to two hours, and they have to drive back, another twenty minutes."

She let out a breath. "So the timing isn't so far off. But Hannah told you that they were going to watch a movie at Lucas's grandmother's place, and she promised to be home by midnight." She shut her eyes for a moment to slow her racing thoughts. "Hannah's a sheltered, naive girl, and what do we really know about Lucas? Is he a careful driver? Does he drink alcohol or smoke pot? We don't even know how much older than Hannah he is."

Tony narrowed his eyes.

"I can tell Hannah really likes him. And he seems like a nice guy, but…if they both like each other…I mean, kids can get carried away."

"Are you sure you're thinking about Hannah and Lucas?"

"Who else would I—" She met his eyes. "They hardly know each other. We knew each other very well. And we were in love."

Tony let out a breath. "Yes, we were."

His admission warmed her deep inside in spite of her worry about Hannah.

A flash of headlights swept the window. *Thank You.* Maggie jumped up. "They're here."

Glancing out the window, Tony climbed to his feet. "They're both out of the car."

"Good."

Tony moved to Maggie's side. "Shall we let them do the talking?"

"Good plan," Maggie agreed.

Hannah pushed open the door and hurried inside, Lucas right behind her. "I'm sorry we're late," Hannah began.

"It was my fault," Lucas said. "I didn't think about how late it would get by the time we got back."

"It's not anybody's fault." Hannah looked from Maggie to Tony. "We tried to get here on time, but Lucas is a safe driver. I mean, you wouldn't want us to drive too fast and have an accident, right?"

"We're sorry to worry you." Lucas' gaze darted from Maggie to Tony and settled on Hannah.

Silence hung in the air for a few heavy seconds. Apparently, they'd both run out of excuses. "How old are you, Lucas?" Maggie asked.

"I'm almost eighteen, ma'am."

Ma'am? Ma'am? Nobody had ever called her ma'am before.

"Old enough to take responsibility for thinking before you act?" Tony asked.

"Yes, sir."

At least, Tony was getting the sir treatment, too.

Tony scowled. "Do you know Hannah's fifteen?"

Lucas nodded.

"Not that you're off the hook, Hannah." Tony frowned at the girl. "You told me you were going to his grandmother's to watch a movie."

Marveling at the authority in Tony's voice, Maggie watched in admiration. If she were either Hannah or Lucas, she'd be shaking in her boots.

"Hannah didn't lie to you." Lucas cleared his throat. "I saw in the paper that the movie I was going to rent was playing in the theater in Dun Harbor, so I changed plans at the last minute. I'm really sorry."

"Do you have a cell phone you would have loaned to Hannah?" Maggie asked.

"Uh…sure."

Maggie focused on the girl. "You should have used

it. Mrs. Stefano promised your parents she'd be responsible for you. Because Mrs. Stefano isn't here, you're my responsibility. You have my cell number. Or you could have called here and run your change in plans by Tony."

"Do you have to tell Mrs. Stefano?" Hannah asked.

"I don't want to worry her, but I will tell your parents. And we called your grandmother, Lucas. She's concerned, too."

"I'd better get home." He looked at Maggie, then Tony. "Are we okay here?"

Maggie frowned uneasily. What she wanted to do was forbid Hannah from anything that didn't involve work or being safe at home, but she needed time to think about it. Besides, she hadn't been spending much time with her since Tony arrived, had she? She needed to stay in closer touch with the girl.

Tony glanced at Maggie, then back to Lucas. "Frankly, the difference in your ages concerns us. And you both lacked good judgment tonight."

"I'll do better," Hannah said. "I promise."

"I will, too," Lucas said contritely.

Tony looked at Maggie. "You think we should spell out the rules?"

We should spell out the rules? "Definitely." She gave him a nod to go ahead.

He gave her a who-me stare for about a second. When she stared blankly back, he turned to Lucas. "While you're with Hannah, no alcohol, no pot, no anything. Clear?"

"Yes, sir. Just so you know, I don't use any of that stuff."

"Good. And you will behave like a gentleman with her at all times."

"Yes, sir."

"He already does," Hannah pointed out.

Tony focused on Maggie. "Then are we good?"

She considered a moment. "Yes, I believe we are."

"As long as you both bear in mind, any repeats of tonight will mean no more seeing each other," Tony added.

"Right," the teens said in unison.

Maggie felt as if she'd watched a master. Not only had Tony jumped in and taken command, he'd let the kids know they hadn't lived up to their responsibility without belittling them. He'd laid out the rules and he'd given them consequences if they didn't live up to them. To say she was impressed would be a huge understatement.

But respect for him couldn't dim the ache of loss in her heart. Their daughter was only six years younger than Hannah. And after tonight, Maggie had no question in her mind, Tony would have made a wonderful dad.

The warm breeze ruffling her hair early Monday morning, Maggie refilled the bowl with kibble and quietly replaced it inside the shed. The mother cat and her kittens were all cuddled together in the box of newspapers. She was dying to handle those little balls of fur.

But she'd wait a little longer. She certainly didn't want to frighten the mother into moving them. And when she could handle the kittens, she'd put a stack of Stella's old towels under them and remove the top one daily to help the mother keep them clean, a tip she'd read on the internet.

Glancing at her watch, she decided she needed to get a move on. She quietly let herself out of the shed, hurried back to her Suburban in the driveway and climbed in behind the wheel. A sheet of yellow paper taped to the dashboard with duct tape caught her attention. In Tony's bold handwriting it said, *Here's my cell number in case you need me.*

He *had* been worried Saturday night when he'd found her helping Eric change his tire. A smile unfurled inside like rose petals. Yesterday, he'd gone to church with her and Hannah again. He really seemed to get into the service. And afterward, he'd even let Hannah persuade him to stay to sample the doughnuts during Fellowship. Maggie liked having him in church with her...a lot.

She reached for her phone and punched in the numbers on the paper. Two rings. She envisioned him climbing over rubble to get to his cell. Or maybe he had to put down the crowbar or his hammer to get the phone from his jeans pocket.

Three rings. "Yeah," he said gruffly.

She struggled to remember why she'd called. Other than to hear his voice, that is. "Thanks for your number."

Heavy silence for a couple beats. "Make sure you use it." His voice had taken on a serious undertone.

"I'm using it right now."

"Where are you?"

"In my Suburban in the driveway."

His low chuckle made her feel warm inside. "While I have you on the phone, will it work if I borrow your truck this afternoon to pick up lumber in Eau Claire?"

"I'll be working at the greenhouse later. I'll leave the keys in the ignition."

"Thanks."

She frowned. "But why are you going to Eau Claire for lumber with Clyde's lumberyard in town?"

"Clyde's? I need lots of lumber, Maggie, not just the few scraps Clyde carries."

"You haven't seen his new place north of town? He stocks almost everything, and he'll order if he doesn't have what you need. Builders around here say his prices are reasonable, too."

"Thanks, I'll give him a call, see if he can help me out. Now get to work."

"Aye, aye, sir."

"And Maggie…"

"Yeah."

"Have a great day." He hung up.

She sat with the receiver to her ear, staring into space. The memory of how she'd felt that day in the attic when she'd realized he was staying jolted through her with ferocious clarity. Drawing in a deep breath, she pushed the End button on the phone, the memory fading in the cold light of reality.

Tony was here now, but for only a couple of months. *Thank You for guiding him to stay awhile. But he'll be leaving as soon as he has Stella's house fit for her to come home.*

Please help me remember the leaving part.

That evening, Maggie sat on Hannah's bed sharing a bowl of popcorn with the teenager and having an overdue girl-talk session. She couldn't help feeling partially responsible for Hannah's lapse the other night. She'd been so focused on Stella and Tony since he'd been home that she'd neglected Hannah. She needed to get back on track with the girl and reestablish the rules her parents had relayed to Maggie during their phone call.

So far, they'd discussed the most flattering shades of lipstick according to Hannah's friends, the importance of wearing sunscreen, Hannah's grade point average and her future plans to go to UW Eau Claire. "I'm glad you're thinking beyond high school, Hannah. You'll be a sophomore this fall, right?"

Hannah nodded. "My older brother says sophomore year is easier than being a freshman."

"Did he say why?"

"He says I'll know what to expect." Hannah sighed. "Freshman year was pretty much up for grabs every day. First semester was like…the worst."

Maggie nodded. "Things are changing so fast, it's hard to figure out where you belong. Is that what you mean?"

Hannah nodded pensively.

One of the things that stood out Maggie's freshman year was her parents' refusal to allow her to date. They said she was too young. But Tony was a junior and he played sports, so he'd been part of homecoming and prom courts which required he take a date. When her parents wouldn't budge, he'd asked Rachel. And Maggie had been beside herself with jealousy and the injustice of the situation.

Looking back, she realized freshman year had been her last year of being a carefree girl. Sophomore year, she'd gone to special classes in Eau Claire with a group of other pregnant girls. She'd do whatever she could to keep Hannah from going that route. "You know, Hannah, when I called your mother, she said you aren't allowed to date yet."

Hannah squinted. "We pretty much hang out in groups…except for a couple people."

"Wouldn't you call going to the movie with Lucas a date?"

"Well, yeah, I guess."

"Different sets of rules is only one reason eighteen and fifteen aren't a good age combination."

"Lucas isn't eighteen yet. Anyway, I might agree with you if I didn't know Lucas. He's great."

"Did you tell him your parents don't allow you to date?"

She shook her head.

"Because you want to be cool?"

"I guess. I really like him, Maggie. He's so cute… plus he's very nice and considerate. He even opens the car door for me."

"Hannah, Lucas has more experience with life. With girls. He drives. He'll be going to college this fall."

"He's going to West Point."

"Really?"

"He's very smart."

"I'm sure he is. But your parents don't let you go out on dates at home, which means I can't let you date here. Your mom agreed you can occasionally watch a movie with Lucas either here or at his grandma's, but that's it."

Hannah frowned, her bottom lip protruding in a pretty pout. "You don't trust us."

Maggie had no intention of letting the conversation go in that direction. "I'm merely following your parents' rules."

"But you're young. I don't think my parents remember being young."

Maggie smiled. "Maybe they regret some of their choices when they were young, and they're trying to keep you from making the same mistakes."

"Like what?"

"I don't know. Maybe you should ask them."

"Do you regret things you did when you were young?"

To the depth of her soul. She sighed. "Yes."

"Like what?"

Maggie shook her head, the ache in her chest making it hard to breathe. She offered Hannah some popcorn, using the moment of distraction to compose herself.

Hannah took a handful. "What things?" she repeated.

"Things I would give anything to change. Unfortunately, I'll never be able to do that." She set down the bowl.

"Did those things involve Tony?"

Maggie jerked to look at the girl. "Why do you ask that?"

"I don't know. You two seem to have something, like, really deep going on between you."

Obviously, Hannah was more observant than Maggie had realized. "We've been friends for a long time. We grew up next door to each other."

"I think…well…it's like you love each other."

Maggie swallowed. She tried to say something, but she couldn't manage the words. The clock on the dresser ticked out the seconds.

Hannah munched her popcorn, the rhythm of her chewing synching with the clock. She watched Maggie, her expression curious and a little dreamy as only a fifteen-year-old could pull off. "Do you think you and Tony will get married someday?"

Maggie shook her head and tried to laugh, not that she succeeded. "That's never going to happen, Hannah."

"Why not?"

"Because Tony and I are very different. For starters, he likes to travel the world, and I love Noah's Crossing. He's just not into family and roots and the things most important to me. We can't change who we are. You'll understand when you get older."

"I thought love was supposed to overcome everything."

Maggie had thought that when she was fifteen, too. "Ideally. Problem is, we live in the real world."

Hannah traced the pattern in the old quilt on her bed, her expression growing more serious. "Maggie, do you believe God has a plan for your life?"

Maggie considered her question. It was hard for her to believe God had planned for her parents to die when she was only a girl and needed them so desperately. She didn't want to accept that God had planned to give her no option but to give away her baby either. She knew she and Tony were responsible for making choices that led down that road.

Looking into Hannah's open, expectant face, Maggie understood she needed to give the girl an answer. And she needed to be honest. "I think we spend our lives making choices. Some good, some not so good. I don't know about anybody else, but I guess I'm still trying to figure out what His plan for me is. Does that make sense?"

"I guess." Hannah nodded. "I know we need to trust Him…no matter what happens. I mean, Job lost everything, and he still trusted God."

This kid thought about Job at fifteen? Maggie didn't know if she even knew who Job was at that age.

"I think God has a plan for everybody even if a person doesn't know what it is," Hannah said with the confidence of youth. "I don't think He wants you to be alone, Maggie. I think His plan is for you and Tony to be together."

Maggie stared at the girl. She had a distinct feeling she was coming out of this conversation with more to think about than Hannah was. So much for her coaching the fifteen-year-old. She only hoped Hannah's thinking carried over to her feelings for Lucas.

And the decisions she might have to make.

Chapter Thirteen

"The black one's a male." On his knees by the box in the shed, Tony gently set the tiny, helpless kitten near his mother. "How about Darth Vader? Vader for short?"

The mother cat began licking her offspring as if checking to make sure he was all right.

Kneeling beside Tony, Maggie petted the mother cat she and Hannah had named Snowball. "What do you think, Mommy? Do you like Vader?"

"I like it." Hannah carefully cuddled the gray kitten with white ears. "I think this sweet little girl should be Whisper."

"Perfect," Maggie agreed. "So the white female with gray boots like the mother is Boots, the all-gray female is Ginger, the gray with white ears is Whisper, the black little guy is Vader."

"And tiger stripe could be Shadow," Hannah said.

"You know…" Maggie gave Tony a little smile. "I think he looks more like a Terminator."

He laughed. "Perfect." He picked up the tiny tabby, noting his little belly was as round as his siblings'. Their mother was doing a great job of feeding her litter.

"Terminator?" Hannah sounded horrified. "But he's so little and sweet."

"Let's hope he grows into his name," Maggie said. "He'll have to keep up with Darth Vader, won't he?"

Hannah shrugged. "I guess." She set Whisper near the mother, who licked the kitten thoroughly. "It must be so weird for them not to see anything, don't you think? How much longer before they open their eyes?"

"Soon. When they're about ten days old." Tony set Terminator down, so the mother could check him out.

"When she's old enough, do you think I can take Whisper home with me, if my mom says it's okay?"

Maggie frowned as if she hadn't considered giving any of them away.

Not that Tony was surprised. Maggie held on. To houses, people and, apparently, kittens. "The vet says they need to nurse for at least eight weeks, but twelve, even fourteen can be beneficial."

Maggie looked relieved.

"But feeding six cats will get expensive," he reminded. "Plus annual shots and stuff."

Maggie sighed. "I read on the internet that because we don't know if the mother was vaccinated or not, we should get that done now. She should also be wormed to protect her and the kittens."

"Neutering all of them will be expensive, too." Tony looked at Hannah. "There's a lot of responsibility that goes with a pet."

Hannah nodded. "But I'm making money this summer."

"Think about it," Maggie said. "If you decide that caring for a kitten is what you want to spend your money on, we'll talk more about it."

Hannah smiled. "Great."

Maggie met Tony's eyes as if she knew very well it was a done deal in the teenager's mind.

"Lucas said his grandma loves cats. Maybe she'd take one, too."

Maggie's head jerked to look at Hannah.

He put his hand on Maggie's shoulder and gave her a smile. "It'll be okay."

But she didn't return his smile. She just looked sad.

You'd think she was contemplating giving away her own child.

Maggie took in a hot, humid breath of attic air as she tapped the nail with her hammer to set it. Holding her breath, she hauled the hammer back and whacked. Yet another nail bent in half. She wanted to stamp her foot. Instead, she impatiently dragged off her leather work gloves. "What is wrong with these things?"

Tony took the hammer from her—again. He grabbed a nail from his tool belt and positioned it on the two-by-four. "Tap it softer to set it." He demonstrated. "Hold off with your super-punch. Just give it a thump to drive it deeper, then haul back and let fly." He drove the nail into the board like a champ and handed the hammer back to her. "Try again."

With a determined huff, she took the hammer from him, pushed at her hard hat, adjusted her eye gear, juggled the hammer from one hand to the other to tug her leather gloves on again and grasped another nail from her tool belt. "These work boots aren't just heavy, they're hot. Are you sure I need all this gear?"

"Yeah. If you step on a nail, it could go right through your tennis shoes. And you need the jeans and long sleeves to keep you from getting scratched and full of slivers. Can't have that, can we?"

"Can't we?"

He squinted. "Ready to work?"

She swiped the back of her hand across her damp forehead. Concentrating fiercely, she set the nail this time, and gave it a measured thump which sank the thing a little more without bending it. Then she drew back and whacked. A few more whacks and the nail was in, nearly straight.

"Good girl." He shot her a half grin.

She liked that grin. And now that she'd experienced a bit of success, she was determined to get serious about helping. After all Tony had done up here, it was the least she could do. She grasped another nail. Placed it, tapped, thumped, whacked—in. Wow.

"You've got it." This time, he gave her the full grin.

She grinned right back.

"I'll cut a support beam." He pointed at the expanse of blue sky overhead. "Think you can help me nail it in place up there?"

"Sure." She took in the height, the ladders at either end of the high dormer, the backyard far, far below. A little dizzy, she focused instead on the new plank floor at her feet. She could do this. Of course she could.

He moved a few steps away, picked up the electric saw and bent over a thick board balanced between two sawhorses. Saw buzzing, it voraciously cut where he guided.

She watched his large, expert hand guide the saw until the power tool stopped making racket. "Okay, Maggie."

She scooted to his side and lifted one end of the long board. It weighed much more than she'd anticipated.

"Too heavy?"

"Nope." Clumsily, she shifted the hammer in her fingers and dropped it into the tool belt she wore.

He strode over to the far ladder, glancing back to check her progress.

She shuffled behind him and stopped at the nearer ladder.

"Careful," he coached, stepping on the bottom rung.

Hanging on to the board with one hand, she grasped her ladder for dear life, lifted her foot, gained the rung, then another and another.

"Good. Don't look down. Now jut the board against that smaller one."

She tried to ignore the view far below as she put all her strength behind hefting the board into place.

"Can you hold it there with one hand and get a nail and your hammer out of your tool belt? Be careful not to lean back and lose your balance."

She leaned her full hundred-ten pounds into one arm to hold the board in place and fumbled in the belt compartment for a nail. Her muscles were so tense they were trembling. How in the world had Tony done all this work by himself? Obviously, those impressive muscles of his weren't just for her to appreciate.

She pounded her nail, and it actually worked. As she got the hang of things, she began to relax a little. They both pounded away, climbing down to move the ladder when need be. Tony pounded nails three-quarters of the way to her quarter, but who was counting?

"You're doing great," he encouraged. "You can finish up the nailing here while I cut another beam." He climbed down and left her hammering.

Apparently, he'd decided she could be trusted not to fall. Humming a little tune, she tapped, thumped and whacked away until she realized the saw was not buzzing. She looked over her shoulder.

He stood, hands on hips, watching her.

"Am I doing something wrong?"

"You're doing great."

She smiled, her legs feeling a little unsteady. Not a good thing, perched on the ladder as she was. "Get to work, Stefano."

"Yes, ma'am." He bent over the sawhorses, the buzz of the machine raking the sweltering air.

She turned back to work, humming her little tune. Finally, she climbed down just as Tony finished sawing. Her legs a tad rubbery, she walked over to grasp another heavy board.

"What is that song you keep humming?" he asked.

"Does it bother you?"

"No, it just sounds familiar. What is it?"

"'Side by Side.'"

He gave her another one of those half grins of his. "Yeah, that's it. You used to sing that a lot when we were kids."

She nodded, happy he remembered.

By the time they'd nailed a bunch of the long, heavy boards in place, Maggie's muscles were weak with fatigue. And it was only 9:00 a.m.

"Let's take a break." He laid his eye gear and hard hat down and shoved a hand through his tousled hair as he peered up at their work. "I couldn't have done that without your nailing the opposite end, Maggie. We make a good team."

"You're a good teacher." She crumpled to the floor, stretching her legs out in front of her and laying her gloves, eye gear and hard hat beside her. The sun shone down through the open roof like a laser.

Tony walked to the stairs and rubbed a towel over his glistening face and hair. He lifted a canteen to his lips, then gave it to her.

Taking it from him, their gazes locked and held. His black eyes seemed to peer into her soul. Would he lean down and kiss her? Her heart did a flip.

Not good. She shouldn't be thinking about kissing him. And her heart should not be so happy that she was. What was wrong with her?

He turned and walked away.

She closed her eyes. Her arms shouldn't be aching to hold him close either.

He couldn't stay. He'd never misled her about that. She drank from the canteen, the liquid cooling her parched throat.

His back to her, he busied himself with details.

She loved watching him work, loved working beside him. In fact, there wasn't a place in the whole world she'd rather be than in this steamy attic…with him.

Tony strode down the rehab center hall, Maggie at his side. He could ride for days with her behind him on the Harley. Or nailing beams beside him like she'd done today. She'd worked like a trooper in the sweltering attic heat, and they'd accomplished a lot.

But the more time they spent together, the tougher it got to keep his emotional distance. He liked being with her. Always had. Even now, he longed to put his arm around her shoulders just to keep her close.

Instead, he followed her into Nonna's room and over to the bed, actually looking forward to seeing his grandmother, especially with Maggie at his side.

Nonna looked better. More energy in her posture. Her room resembled a flower shop, plants and vases of flowers setting everywhere, their mingled scents filling the room.

With a soft flutter, Maggie bent, hugged the older woman and planted a kiss on both her offered cheeks. The women smiled at each other with so much affection his throat closed. Maggie stepped back to allow him access.

He bent and wrapped his arms around Nonna in a gentle hug.

"Caro," she murmured in his ear. "Maggie tells me you are working night and day on the house. But I miss you when you do not come to see me."

Her endearment warmed him. She'd missed him? He wanted to believe she meant it. Straightening, he glanced at Maggie.

Her mouth softened in a smile. She had such a glow about her.

Tearing his eyes away, he set the pie he'd been carrying on the bedside table. "Della sent a rhubarb pie for you, Nonna, to celebrate the birth of Rachel's twins." And he'd stuffed another donation in Della's jar for the hungry. A satisfactory exchange for both of them, he supposed.

"I stopped in to see Rachel and her babies yesterday. They are so adorable," Maggie said.

"Please convey my congratulations. And my thanks to Della." Nonna looked from Tony to Maggie and back again as she drew herself up a little straighter. "You both look tired...but very happy."

Now that Nonna mentioned it, under Maggie's radiance, she did look a little tired. She'd worked too hard. But didn't she always throw herself totally into whatever she did? "Maggie helped me work in the attic today."

"Ah. How are the repairs coming along?"

Repairs? More like a complete overhaul. Maggie must be playing down the demolition to keep Nonna from worrying about it. He decided to change the subject. "Things are good. How is your therapy going?"

"Jim says I am mastering the walker."

"Fantastic."

"What does Dr. Peterson say?" Maggie sounded jubilant.

"He says I cannot go to the dairy breakfast tomorrow. And I must build more strength in my muscles before I can come home. Perhaps two weeks."

"Two weeks?" Tony stared at his grandmother. He hadn't believed she'd ever come home, but Maggie had. He'd never been more glad to be proven wrong. "That's great!"

Maggie grasped Nonna's hand. "I'm so glad."

Tony ran a quick mental check of all the things that had to be done to make the house functional for a woman with a walker. The most looming problem was the half-finished downstairs bathroom, but getting the roof on was even more urgent. He'd accomplished a lot over the past couple weeks in the attic while he had daylight and in the downstairs bathroom at night.

But even if he worked around the clock with Maggie helping him whenever she could… "I don't think we can get the house ready in two weeks."

Both women focused on him as if he'd alighted from a distant planet. "Of course it will be ready," Maggie said. "If not completely, we'll do some improvising."

Improvising? He opened his mouth to ask her how you improvised a roof and a bathroom, glanced at Nonna, decided to hold his tongue. Probably best not to spoil the celebration. He could worry silently, he guessed. He was beginning to get used to worrying lately, almost resigned to it.

"I will make do," Nonna said. "My home always gives me what I truly need."

Another thing Maggie had been right about.

Maggie laid her small hand on his arm and smiled her soft, radiant smile. "Stella and I will choose fresh wallpaper for the little room off the kitchen."

"Your office? No," Nonna protested.

"I've been thinking about moving my office into my old house." Maggie focused on Tony. "Thanks for giving me the idea."

Tony couldn't help smiling. She'd listened to his idea more than he thought.

"The room will make a perfect bedroom, Stella. We'll put a commode in the closet if the bathroom isn't ready. The most important thing is getting the ramp built so you can get into the house."

The ramp she'd been trying to build the day he'd arrived. She'd had her priorities straight then, too. He guessed everything would come together eventually. Anything seemed possible when Maggie smiled that smile.

Grinning like a fool, he cast good sense aside and plunged right in. "You concentrate on getting well, Nonna. We'll have the house ready for you."

Maggie's smile turned dazzling.

He knew he had a silly grin planted on his face, but he didn't know how to squelch it. All he could do was drink her in. He really needed to get a grip.

"I must discuss something with you, Anthony." Nonna's voice came as if from a distance. "Maggie, if you will find an aide and ask her for plates and forks, we will share Della's pie."

Maggie gave him an I-don't-have-any-idea-what-this-is-about shrug and glided away.

He wanted to follow her. He missed her hand on his arm. He didn't want to experience the emptiness of the room without her in it. Trying to figure out what he'd done to warrant Nonna's need to talk to him alone, he turned to face her.

She studied him narrowly.

The look that said he was about to get the third degree, and he'd better come up with the right answers because she already knew what those answers should be. Oddly, his stomach knotted just as it had when he was a kid. "What is it, Nonna?"

"I have been putting my affairs in order."

He frowned, not sure he was following her. "But you're doing better, aren't you?"

"Much better. But it is time for me to update such things. I am almost eighty years old, Anthony. Even *I* cannot live forever."

"I hope you'll be around for a long time, Nonna."

"It will not matter to you whether I am around or not unless you stay."

He narrowed his eyes. She never changed her tune. "Nonna…I'm staying until I get the house fixed up. That's all I can manage."

She shook her head. Obviously, he'd given her the wrong answer. Again. "Does Maggie know you plan to leave?"

"Of course she knows."

Shaking her head, she patted the bed beside her.

He sat where she'd indicated.

She reached for his hand and clasped it tightly. "Who will take care of her when you're gone? When I'm gone?"

He shook his head. "That's not going to happen for a long time."

"And when it does, who will she have?"

He attempted to ignore the knot tightening in his stomach. "She's pretty good at taking care of herself."

"She is. But she has no family."

"She has you and Hannah."

"Anthony…"

"Practically the whole town is her family."

"But she needs a good man."

He squinted at her. Nonna had moved him into her "good man" category? She'd even attached taking care of Maggie to it? Wouldn't competent, independent Maggie be thrilled Nonna thought she needed a man to take care of her?

"Jim has been Maggie's trusted adviser through my illness. I don't know what she would have done without him. And I can see he's grown to care for our Maggie. He's kind, considerate and would be very good for her."

Feeling sick, Tony clenched his jaw. Nonna had her physical therapist lined up for Maggie?

"Have you nothing to say, Anthony?"

"What do you want me to say?"

"Perhaps the obvious…that Jim is not right for Maggie."

Tony's sentiments exactly.

"You and Maggie were so close as children, and I see how you look at each other now. It is clear you are meant to be together."

Tony swallowed, his throat dry as sandpaper.

"That's why I have willed my house to the two of you."

"What?" He shook his head. "I don't want the house. Give it to Maggie."

She smiled. "I am very happy you want to take care of her. It confirms how you feel about her."

He wasn't about to let her bait him. He'd definitely missed something.

"You think I don't notice you are in love with her?"

He stared at his grandmother. Growing up, he'd often suspected she could read him like a book. Was she right about Maggie? Was he still in love with her? No question, he admired her, loved being with her, couldn't stop smiling when she was near. But…love? As…in love?

"I could not be more pleased." She patted his hand.

She was pleased?

"Now you will stay and make her happy."

"I've never stayed anywhere, Nonna."

Her eyes widened in apparent surprise. "You will take her away with you?"

He couldn't keep up with these huge leaps Nonna was making. His head was still ringing with her first statement. Was he in love with Maggie?

"Anthony? You will take Maggie with you?"

"She'd never be happy on my construction sites. She's totally into making a success of her businesses. Plus she'd miss you and people in Noah's Crossing."

"You wouldn't leave her."

He grabbed on to the side of the bed as if that would keep this conversation from spinning out of control. "Nonna, Maggie knows I'm going back. I was always going back."

She pursed her lips and glowered as if she couldn't understand. "You criticize your papa for leaving you behind, but he never left his Celia."

"He married my mother."

"And you will not marry Maggie?"

Chest heavy, he shut his eyes against her accusing

tone. Marriage had never crossed his mind as a possibility. Not for him. He did his best to clear his head. And reached for reality. "Maggie doesn't need me any more than you do."

"What?" Nonna pressed her fingers to her forehead. "I have never needed you?"

Swallowing, he shook his head.

Nonna closed her eyes for a long moment. Finally, she opened them and met his gaze. "When Salvatore died, I grieved deeply. For him and for me. I was all alone, you see. You and your parents never came home. Salvatore's and my families were in Italy. I thought about moving to be near them, but I could not leave the life Salvatore and I had built in America." Tears filled her eyes. "I wanted desperately to join him in death."

He hated seeing her like this. He'd hurt her. He hadn't meant to, but he had. Why else would she be putting herself through memories of that horrible time? He clasped her hand. "I'm sorry, Nonna. Don't think about that time."

"You must understand, Anthony. After Salvatore and your mother died, it was as if the light in the family had gone out. We had all lost our happiness. Grief was unbearable."

He blew out a breath, his own eyes moist. "Please, Nonna, this isn't good for you."

"But I must explain to you. When your father brought you home to me, you became my reason to go on. My reason for living, really. I needed you more than I should have." She raised his hand to her lips and kissed it. "And I still need you."

He swallowed. His chest feeling like it might explode, he rubbed his fingers against his jaw. How had he gotten things so wrong about her? Had he held on to the pain and resentments of a little boy and never even thought to consider things might be more complicated than he remembered? That they might be different? "I love you, Nonna."

A soft smile lit her face. "I love you, too, my child. More than you can possibly know."

Chapter Fourteen

The hazy sun hovered on the horizon, anticipating its dive behind the curve of the earth. Wind buffeted Maggie on the motorcycle, an occasional bug pinged off the helmet visor covering her face and she had the sensation she was flying through space on a low rocket. All she could do was keep her arms around Tony and hang on for dear life.

He'd seemed distracted while they ate pie with Stella. Now she could feel the tension in his muscles, and he was going faster than usual. What had his nonna talked to him about?

The roar of the motorcycle was too loud to ask. But as soon as she stepped on terra firma again, she was going to find out.

He turned into the driveway, stopped and sat there, motorcycle vibrating.

She waited for him to switch off the engine and lights.

"You can climb off," he yelled over the idling machine. "I'm going for a ride."

Apparently, Stella had brought up things he wanted to think over. But he was too preoccupied to go riding off by himself. Besides, he probably wouldn't come back until after she was in bed, which meant she wouldn't get any answers tonight about his talk with Stella. Not gonna happen. "I'll go with you," she yelled back.

He turned his head to look at her. "You're too scared."

"Not anymore."

"I have the bruised ribs to prove it."

She gave him the I'm-onto-you look that always got results. "You're trying to get rid of me?"

"Hang on." He took off out of the driveway.

Success, of sorts. He hadn't left her behind, but now, she was flying through the twilight, hanging on for her life again.

The engine of the giant machine droned on, mile after mile after mile. Dusk faded to evening. All she could do was relax, trust he'd keep them safe and hold him close, as if he belonged to her.

Finally, he pulled onto a narrow, gravel service road along Rainbow Lake, stopped and shut off the motor and lights. The lap of the waves on the lake and the din of frogs and crickets filled the night.

Drawing in the fresh scent of the spring-fed lake, she looked around. Lights from the few houses along the shoreline reflected off the water, but with the moon playing hide-and-seek with the clouds, it was too dark to see much else. "What are we doing here?"

"Not sure. But as long as we are, let's see if the old diving platform is still hanging in the tree."

"Where is it?"

"A mile or so ahead."

"I'll come with you, provided my legs ever stop vibrating, so I can crawl off this thing. Of course, then there will be standing on them." She unwound her arms and maneuvered herself off the machine.

He climbed off, too, and towered over her as if ready to pick up the pieces if need be.

"I'm standing," she said in triumph. She removed the heavy helmet and handed it to him, then shook out her hair.

He stood there, watching her, a questioning look on his face.

"What?" she asked.

He squinted and shook his head. "Nothing. Just trying to figure something out, that's all." He hung the helmet on the handlebar and started walking down the road.

She hustled to catch up with him. "You're trying to figure out something you and Stella talked about?"

He gave a nod.

"Can I help?"

"Not on this." He gave her a sympathetic look. "Sorry."

Why wouldn't he tell her? Their shoes scuffing gravel mingled with the night sounds of the lake. A slice of moon peeked out from the clouds. "Did she seem worried about something?"

He grunted.

Not a very enlightening response either.

He pointed. "You see any sign of a platform in one of those trees out there?"

She peered at the outlines of trees. "I don't see anything."

"The trees along the road are taller. Maybe we can catch a glimpse by the lake." He veered off the road.

She followed him down the embankment and wound with him through a stand of cottonwoods, the ground soft underfoot. Leaves rustled as little critters ran for cover and the gentle lap of the water grew more pronounced. "Do you know where we are?"

"There's a cove ahead. At least there used to be. We should be able to see the platform from there."

The frogs stopped singing in unison as if an alarm had been transmitted that humans were approaching. "You sure we aren't trespassing?"

"Not sure at all."

Okay, then. Wasn't she glad she asked? "Tony, you have to tell me what Stella talked to you about."

He picked up his pace, a twig snapping under his boot.

She hurried to keep up.

"She told me about her will."

She hated even thinking about Stella's will. "She explained she gave her roses to me?"

"What?"

"The roses. She gave them to me. She said she had it put in her will."

"Great."

"Do you mind?"

"Why would I mind? You love those roses. You should have the roses." He stopped so quickly she almost ran into him. "This is the cove." He lowered his voice. "There's a house around the bend. See the glow of the lights?"

"Yes." Lights sparkled and rippled on the black water like fireflies.

"That house is standing on the hill where the big tree used to be."

For some reason, she felt sad. "The platform's gone then."

"Looks that way."

"We girls used to hear you guys from the swimming beach. You sounded like you were having a lot of fun. One time, Dixie and I set out to find you, but we got lost in the woods."

"Probably just as well. Looking back, that platform wasn't the safest thing, but the guys thought it was cool. We wanted adventure. Nobody telling us what to do. Wild and free."

"Apparently, you like some things from your past."

"Guess so."

A loon called plaintively from the lake.

"So what about Stella's will are you trying to figure out?"

He dragged a breath and took his time to answer. "She thinks willing the house to both of us will make me stay."

"No, the house should be yours."

"I don't want it." He turned to her. "I've never considered that house to be my home."

"Where is your home?"

He shrugged.

"I thought my home would always be where I'd lived with my parents. Maybe that's why I've never done anything with it. But since you asked me about setting up the offices there, I've been thinking…it's only a vacant house. It's not my home anymore—love doesn't live there. Maybe your nonna wants to give you a home where love lives."

He leveled his gaze on her as if he had something important to say. "She told me she needs me. That she's always needed me."

Chills danced over Maggie's skin, tears burning her eyes.

"Why didn't I know that, Maggie?" He rubbed the

back of his neck. "I figured I'd let everybody down. Nonna, you, your parents. He stared out at the water and pressed his lips into a line. "I hadn't hurt Doc or stolen his money, but I knew people would take the sheriff's word over mine. I believed everybody would be better off without me."

"Oh, Tony." She laid her hand on his chest and looked deeply into his eyes. "Nobody felt that way. We loved you. We needed you. I needed you. You don't know how much."

He stroked his hand over her shoulder and pulled her to him.

She laid her head on his chest, slipped her arms around his waist. He smelled of fresh air, rhubarb pie and Tony.

He folded her close. Stroking her hair, he raised her chin and gazed into her eyes. The night hushed as if time stood still. He bent closer and tenderly touched his lips to hers.

Melting against him, she kissed him back with years of longing.

When he ended the kiss, he burrowed his face against her neck and held her close.

She could feel his heart thudding in unison with hers. She was exactly where she wanted to be. In Tony's arms. And whether he was staying or not, there was no use denying she was still in love with him.

How could she deny something as natural as the rain?

Tony held Maggie close, his heart pounding like a jackhammer. When had he decided to kiss her? He didn't know. But now that he had, he wanted to go on holding her, kissing her until the end of time.

He dragged a breath of her fresh scent and kissed her neck. He needed her in so many ways. Ways that scared him to death. He needed her smile, her encouragement, her belief in him. He needed her sense of humor, her teasing, her determination to set the world right. He even needed her logic glitches.

But he had serious thinking to do regarding his feelings for Maggie. He made himself raise his head.

She met his gaze, as if words weren't needed.

He'd never been so close to another human being. Never felt so much admiration or respect. Never been so fulfilled, yet so in need. So proud, yet so humble. So invincible, yet so vulnerable.

Whenever she was near, he was aware of every breath she took. Every expression on her lovely face. Every subtle shift of her body. He came alive in a way he'd never experienced before. The world was a brighter place with more good things in it than he'd ever realized. The sky bluer, the air sweeter. Everything took on a whole new meaning.

Nonna was right. He'd never stopped loving Maggie McGuire.

But what was he going to do about it? *That* he didn't know. Silently, he released her, clasped her hand, and they walked slowly back to the Harley, the air filled with questions needing to be answered.

But one thing he was sure of. He had no right to tell her he loved her unless he loved her enough to stay.

When Maggie and Tony arrived home, she relinquished holding him close and headed for the door. They'd both been deep in thought since those tender moments by the lake. So much had passed between them without saying a word.

She loved him, but she didn't hold out much hope they could ever be together. Her home was here. And even if Tony loved her, too, he still loved his work and traveling around the world.

Not to mention the fact that he hated Noah's Crossing.

Letting herself in the door, she realized the house was dark. Had Hannah told her about plans for this evening? She didn't think so. She glanced at her watch. Eleven o'clock. But Hannah was a night owl who puttered around way past eleven before she went to bed.

"Hannah?" Maggie called up the stairs. The girl didn't answer. Maggie ran up the steps and knocked on her bedroom door. Still no answer. She opened the door and peeked in. The bed hadn't been slept in. She turned and flew down the steps. "Hannah's not in her room."

Tony looked up from his laptop at the kitchen table. "She didn't say she was going anywhere?"

"No. And it's after eleven."

He grasped his cell from his belt, found a number in his list and clicked on it. "I'm calling Lucas's grandmother." He switched the phone to speaker.

"Hello," the older woman said tentatively.

"This is Tony Stefano. I'm sorry for calling so late, but I'd like to speak to Lucas, please."

"I'm sorry. Lucas isn't home."

"Do you know if he's with Hannah?"

"Why, yes. He said Hannah was taking part of the day off work, and they were going to dinner and a movie in Eau Claire."

Maggie shook her head, anger flashing. When they hadn't seen Hannah at the diner earlier, she'd assumed the girl was washing dishes in the back room. Did

Hannah really think they'd let her get away with blatantly disobeying her parents' rule?

"The problem is, she didn't ask permission," Tony said. "When did Lucas leave?"

"I believe it was close to three o'clock."

Maggie heard a car in the drive. "I think they just pulled in." She raced to the window.

Tony strode behind her. "They're here. Lucas will be home very soon."

"I'm sorry for the trouble."

"Thanks. So are we."

Maggie threw open the door just as the teenagers hit the porch. "Hannah, where have you been?"

"We tried to call, but nobody was home and I couldn't get you on your cell either," she sputtered. "Besides, we're only ten minutes late."

Hardly able to believe Hannah's pathetic attempt to deny doing wrong, Maggie wanted to shake her. Instead, she glared at the girl. "You are wrong on so many levels."

"We witnessed an accident and had to wait for the police," Lucas explained. "We would have been here well before eleven if not for that. Honest."

"That's not the problem. Hannah's parents do not want her going on unsupervised dates," Tony said.

Lucas frowned at Hannah. "You said everything was okay."

"You don't understand," Hannah pleaded.

"You didn't tell them?"

"They never would have let me go."

Lucas gave Tony and Maggie a very serious look. "I'm sorry we worried you."

"I'm sorry I didn't tell you," Hannah whined.

"An apology isn't enough this time, Hannah," Maggie warned. "But you've explained yourself, Lucas."

Tony nodded. "You're off the hook."

"Thanks." He gave Hannah a fleeting frown. "I have to go." With that, he turned and left.

"Lucas." The door closed behind him. For a moment, Hannah stared at it as if still trying to figure out a way to save the situation. Then she burst into tears. "I hope you're happy. Now he hates me, and he's leaving tomorrow. I'll never see him again."

"Give yourself a couple of years to grow up enough to take responsibility for your actions. There will be plenty of time for dating." He gave Maggie a look. "At least she's safe."

"Not yet, she isn't." She shook her head at Hannah. "I'm so disappointed in you. I can't believe you deliberately lied."

"I didn't lie," Hannah insisted.

"You lied by omission. I'm going to call your parents and tell them to come and take you home."

Hannah whirled to face Maggie. "All right, I shouldn't have done what I did, but I'll never regret having time with Lucas. We didn't do anything we'll regret like you did when you were young. Somehow, I thought you might understand."

Hannah was turning Maggie's admission the other night against her? Wanting to sink through the floor, she glanced at Tony.

He narrowed his eyes as if trying to figure out what Hannah was talking about. "I think you should go to bed, Hannah," he said curtly.

Hannah grasped Maggie's arm. "Please don't call my parents. I won't give you any more trouble. I just wanted time with Lucas before he leaves."

Maggie knew what it was like to want to spend every waking moment with someone. But she couldn't just cave in. Hannah needed to learn a lesson about being deceitful.

Really, Maggie? Hannah's being deceitful? Maybe you should take the plank out of your own eye before you try to remove the speck from hers. The irony of teaching Hannah a lesson about being less than honest when it was exactly what she was doing with Tony hit her full force. What a hypocrite she was.

"Please, Maggie. My parents will make me come right home, I know they will. But I want to stay here and earn more money. Please, will you both forgive me? I was wrong, and I promise I won't give either of you one second of worry from here on out. Please, please don't call my parents." Hannah dissolved into sobs that shook her entire body, tears running down her face and dripping off her chin. She was out of control as only a teenage girl could be.

Maggie couldn't help feeling sorry for her. And she had asked for forgiveness. Who was Maggie to deny her that? And what right did she have to punish the girl when she was just as guilty? She looked at Tony.

His eyes were wide, unbelieving. He was, obviously, horrified by Hannah's out-of-control behavior. Poor guy didn't have a clue what to do.

Maggie figured a hug was what Hannah needed more than anything. She strode over to the girl and stretched her arms out to her.

Hannah collapsed against her.

Waiting for Hannah's sobs to ease, Maggie stroked her hair. "Hannah, I forgive you. And if you keep your promise, I won't call your parents."

Hannah's sobs slowed and gradually stopped. "Thank you." She looked self-consciously at Tony. "I'm sorry."

Looking from Maggie to Hannah as if he had no understanding of what had just happened, he ripped tissues from the box on the counter and handed them to Hannah.

"Thanks." She mopped her face. "Thank you both for believing in me again. This time, I won't let you down." A little sob betraying her, Hannah turned and headed for the stairs. "I'm gonna…you know…" Tears starting again, she pointed upstairs. "G'night."

"Good night," Maggie and Tony said in unison.

Tony brushed his fingers over Maggie's arm in a supportive gesture. "Good job," he murmured.

"Thank you. You, too," she said shakily. She had to tell him what she'd been keeping from him. She needed to find the right words.

"The dairy breakfast is early, right? I'll be there about seven?"

"Yes." Bracing herself, she turned to him. She had to find the words to tell him the truth.

Upstairs, Hannah's bedroom door slammed.

Maggie jumped at the sound.

"You okay?" Tony looked concerned.

She gave him a nod. But she wasn't okay. Not okay at all. She was exhausted, utterly wrung out by the roller coaster of emotion the night had turned into.

Chapter Fifteen

Bright and early next morning, Tony pulled the Harley to a stop behind a long row of cars beside the road, hit the kill switch and lifted his helmet from his head.

Strains of a polka band beckoned from an open field beyond the barn where two enormous white tents stood, side flaps rolled up. People milled everywhere, the hum of voices mingling with tuba and concertina and the squeals of little kids running in circles with a yellow Lab and a couple of frisky border collies.

Tony's mouth watered at the smell of eggs and pancakes and sausage blended with steaming coffee. He'd worked up a huge appetite pounding in the attic since Maggie left this morning.

Funny, he'd assumed there would be about a dozen farmers standing around drinking coffee, complaining about what the weather was doing to their crops, even if everybody knew very well the growing season had been as close to perfect as it got. But it looked as if all of Noah's Crossing and half the county had turned out for the breakfast.

How would he find Maggie in this crowd?

Maggie.

He smiled just thinking about her. But an uneasiness eclipsed his euphoria. He couldn't get Hannah's comment out of his mind. *We didn't do anything we'll regret like you did when you were young.* There were no two ways to read that. And he couldn't erase the look on Maggie's face when she'd gone off to bed. Fear? Dread? It seemed more than just her worries about Hannah. Deeper, somehow. It made no sense last night. Still didn't.

Squinting into the early-morning sun, he strode up the gravel driveway past the white farmhouse decked out with green shutters and window boxes full of flowers and vines trailing almost to the ground. His boots crunching new gravel, he passed a giant pole barn, probably housing machinery. He headed for the barn with its new roof and twin, rooster-crested cupolas. Obviously, Phillips had found a way to make farming lucrative.

In the shade of one of the tents, people sat visiting and chowing down at long tables covered with checkered tablecloths. Searching for Maggie, he almost plowed into Clyde from the lumberyard.

"You found anybody yet to haul those roof trusses you bought from Harold?" Clyde asked.

"Not yet, but thanks for sending me to Harold. I saved a bundle on those recycled trusses. I can handle the hauling, though."

"Alone?"

Truth was, Tony didn't have a clue how he was going to manage, but Clyde had already done more than enough to help. "I'll figure out something."

"You deserve a leg up for taking good care of your grandmother."

A leg up sounded better than charity, he supposed.

Still, he didn't like feeling so helpless and needy. "I'll manage. Thanks. You seen Maggie?"

"In the display tent." Clyde pointed.

"Thanks, catch you later." Tony strode across the rough field, returning hiyas and how-you-doings on the way. He knew some of the people. Others just seemed to assume he belonged there.

The display tent held lines of booths and tons of people, their voices rising and falling in a jumble of neighborliness. Posters and signs advertised everything from puppies to crafts and baked goods and produce. And of course, plants and flowers.

Bright yellow signs covered with eight-by-tens of landscapes and flowers announced 'Scapes by Design and Magnolia's Blossoms. Directly beneath the signs, he spotted copper curls bobbing in conversation.

People and commotion disappeared as he walked toward her, intent on covering the ground between them.

She wore a green dress that usually gave her brown eyes pizazz, but today, her eyes were rimmed with red as if she hadn't slept last night. Or had been crying. Looked like whatever was wrong last night was still bothering her.

She raised her hand in greeting. "Hi," she said.

"Hi, yourself."

"How's work on your grandmother's Victorian coming along, Tony?"

Seemed most of Noah's Crossing knew what he was doing. He turned to the tall, lean man in jeans and blue plaid shirt Maggie had been talking to. Good old Jim, Nonna's physical therapist and Maggie's trusty adviser on all things medical. "The work is moving slower than I'd like."

"Stella sure is fired up to get home," Jim said.

"Sure is." About run out of conversation, Tony glanced at Maggie.

She bit her lip, worry in her eyes.

Tony frowned, anxious for Jim to leave so he could ask Maggie what was wrong.

Jim cleared his throat. "I guess I'd better pay Della for that chocolate pie she put my name on. See you."

"Yeah." Tony gave the guy a parting glance.

Maggie laid her hand on Jim's arm. "Thank you for stopping by."

"Sure." Jim walked slowly away, a resigned look on his face.

Tony almost felt sorry for the guy. Loving Maggie was a hard thing to live with. He fought the urge to haul her into his arms to prove to Jim and everybody else she belonged to *him.* Instead, he met her eyes. "You feeling okay?" he asked.

Her eyes flinched. She swallowed as if she had something she wanted to tell him.

"Morning, Maggie."

"Morning, Sheriff," she said.

Great. Good old Sheriff Bunker. Another one of his favorite people. If he was ever going to find out what Maggie was worrying about, he was going to have to get her away from all these interruptions.

"Good to see you, Tony," Bunker said.

Tony frowned. Had he heard right?

"I hear you're doing right by your grandmother." The sheriff stuck out his hand.

Tony stared at it, considered shaking it, decided to be honest instead. "I think you owe me an apology for accusing me of assaulting and robbing Doc Tilbert ten years ago."

Lowering his hand, Bunker squinted. "I never apologize for doing my job."

Tony should have known the man wouldn't be able to wrap his small mind around an apology.

"Planning to stay long?" Bunker asked.

"As long as I need to."

"I'll probably see you around then." The sheriff walked away.

Tony glared after him.

Maggie touched his hand. "He doesn't just enforce the law, Tony. He thinks he *is* the law. Everybody knows it."

"Then why do people keep electing him sheriff?"

"They credit him with the fact that we have very little crime."

"Maybe he *is* good for something." Not that he'd ever like the man. But as long as he was being honest, if Sheriff Bunker's accusation hadn't given him the push to leave town years ago, wouldn't he have found something else?

"You should have seen the look on your face when he wanted to shake your hand."

"You could have knocked me over with a feather." He clasped her hand, her skin warm and smooth. "Can we get out of here? I'm starving."

"Just a minute." Turning on her heel, she walked over to her display to say something to a young woman, then came back to him and slipped her arm through his. "Let's go get some breakfast."

They began pushing through the crowd toward the smell of food. He loved feeling her at his side, loved the rush of adrenaline being near her gave him. But something was off, and he needed to find out what it was.

"Leave with me after we eat. We'll take the day off together."

"The benefit will last a couple more hours, and then I need to help clean up. I'll meet you at home then. Actually, I...I need to talk to you." She looked very serious.

He nodded. "Good." She wasn't having second thoughts about that kiss last night, was she? Was that what was bothering her? He hoped not. He didn't want to talk about that kiss. He wanted to repeat it. "I'll pack a picnic to take to the lake. Let's just swim and soak up the sun this afternoon."

She gave him a little frown. "We'll see how we feel after we talk, okay?"

That comment did nothing to ease his mind.

"Tony, just the guy I want to see."

Dragging his gaze from Maggie's frown, he turned to face Harold Phillips.

"Did you find anybody to haul those roof trusses?" Harold asked.

"Not yet. You anxious to get them off your place?"

"It's not that." Harold hitched up his jeans. "Me and my sons will bring them over when you need them. Just give me a call."

"Oh?" When Tony bought the trusses, Harold had stipulated that Tony was responsible for delivery. "How much will it cost me?"

"Delivery's included."

Surprised, Tony decided not to look a gift horse in the mouth. "I appreciate it."

"I've got a stack of pretty good lumber taking up space in my machine shed, too. If you can use it, I'll bring it along."

"How much do you need for it?"

Harold shook his head. "It's not for sale. Neither is my labor. My sons' either. I figure you're going to need some able bodies to help you get those trusses in place."

At a total loss for words, Tony stared at the man. "Why are you doing all this?"

"Clyde just told me you need those trusses for Stella Stefano's house. She fed our family for weeks when a tornado took our farm last year. I'd appreciate it if you'd let us help."

So Harold wanted to repay Nonna for her help when he and his family had needed it. Feeling humbled and very grateful, Tony thrust his hand to pump Harold's. "I sure could use it."

"I'll spread the word. Good people are always glad to help out a neighbor when they can. That's how things work around here." Harold slapped him on the back and walked away.

Tony stared after him in amazement. "What just happened?"

"Only being neighborly." Maggie gave him a pinched little smile.

"Tony…"

He turned to see Clyde Billings again.

"I've been thinking…I met a young guy the other day who moved here from Chicago. He's trying to build a house for him and his daughter on Rainbow Lake. Trouble is, he's a newspaperman. Owns the *Courier*. And I get the idea he doesn't know much about building. I was wondering…you think you could find the time to talk to him, maybe give him some pointers?"

Tony squinted. Apparently, Clyde figured Tony knew what he was doing. He liked that the man wasn't just handing out charity, but giving him an opportunity to help someone else, to pay Clyde's help forward. "Sure. I'd be happy to help. I'll stop out there."

"Good." Clyde gave him a thump on the shoulder. "His name is Ben Cooper." With a nod to Maggie, he walked away.

"If you keep impressing everybody around here, they're going to make you stay in Noah's Crossing," Maggie said.

He reached for some variation of his usual quip about the town. *Over my dead body. A fate worse than death.* But he couldn't get the words past his lips.

Somehow, he didn't feel like the same man he'd been when he'd thought those things. He was so tired of being that man. So tired of going it alone.

Maggie gave him a questioning look. "Don't look so worried. I'm teasing."

He nodded. But he didn't much feel like teasing back.

He loved her with his whole heart. She had helped him make peace with the confusion and anger that had weighed him down. Had given him a reason to anticipate each new day, had helped him realize how satisfied he could be working with his hands again. She'd made him feel loved. And freed him to love her.

He had been asking himself the wrong question. He'd been asking himself if he could stay. The real question was how could he leave? "You know, for the first time in my life, staying in Noah's Crossing with you is beginning to look like it could be really good."

Maggie's smile went out. She looked...stunned. "Teasing me about staying is not something you can do, Tony."

He held her gaze. "I've never been more serious."

Frowning, she shook her head.

Not even close to the reaction he'd been going for.

* * *

Maggie's entire system shifted into overdrive, her mind flying in a hundred directions at the same time. Tony really said he was considering staying in Noah's Crossing? With her?

But of course he wouldn't. Would he?

But there he was, smiling down at her, waiting for her to respond in a sane, rational manner. Impossible.

Dear God, I love him. But she'd never dared dream he'd consider staying here with her. Never dreamed there was any hope they could build a long-term relationship. She couldn't go on being dishonest one more minute. She had to tell him about the baby right now.

She glanced around. She couldn't tell him in the middle of all these people. They needed someplace private where nobody would interrupt them. Grasping his hand, she strode out of the tent with him in tow. "We need to talk."

"My bike is that way."

She gave her head a shake and kept walking.

"Where are we going?"

"To that little woods ahead. I have something very important I need to tell you."

Tony walked beside her, his head down. "You don't want me to stay?"

"You know better than that. But…maybe you won't want to."

He pulled her around to face him. "Why wouldn't I want to?"

She glanced back to the tents. "We're almost there, Tony."

He silently let her lead him.

Panic threatened to overwhelm her. She'd prayed most of the night, and she still didn't know how to tell him. *Please give me the words. Please help him understand. Please keep him from blaming himself. Please let him blame me instead of himself.*

Finally, the smell of cool, damp earth enveloped them, and trees shaded them from the sun and from curious eyes. Normally a place of respite, but not today. Today, the glen held an ominous, foreboding quality.

Gathering her strength, Maggie turned to Tony. She looked into his trusting face and pushed on. "When you went away…I didn't know how to find you. And I had something very important you needed to hear."

His eyes winced as if anticipating the pain her words would inflict. "Tell me."

Feeling pain, she realized she was twisting her necklace around her fingers so tightly that she was cutting off her circulation. Breathing in, breathing out, she slowly unwound the chain. When the locket was free, she grasped it and snapped it open. With shaking fingers, she held it up for Tony to see. "This baby isn't me, Tony."

He looked at the tiny picture, then frowned at her, confusion in his eyes. "Who is it?"

Her heart pounded so hard she had trouble breathing. "This is the only picture I have—" a sob betrayed her "—of our beautiful baby girl."

Chapter Sixteen

The tiny picture wavered before Tony's eyes. He tried to take a breath, but his lungs seemed to have shut down.

He looked at Maggie. All he saw was the torture in her tear-filled eyes. All he heard was the pain in her voice.

He struggled to wrap his mind around her words. *Our beautiful baby girl.*

Oh, God. Please. No. Maggie had been only fifteen. Fifteen. He couldn't find words. He pulled her into his arms.

She slipped her arms around his waist and clung to him.

"You were just a kid."

"Oh, Tony…" Sobs shook her body.

He held on to her, wanting to absorb her pain. But he felt numb. He wanted to deny her words. Pretend she hadn't said them. That they weren't real.

Our beautiful baby girl.

She'd said the words, all right. He squeezed his eyes closed, but he couldn't stop his tears from leaking through. *Oh, God. What have I done?* "I'm so sorry, Maggie."

His words sounded lame. Pathetic, really. What good were words?

"I had to give her away," she whispered.

Pressing his forehead to hers, he nodded dumbly, a wave of pain rendering him speechless. Where was he when she'd needed him so desperately?

"That's why I was living with Mom's aunt in Eau Claire when my parents were killed."

It made no sense. "Why?"

"To attend classes with other pregnant girls. They gave us counseling to help us decide whether to keep our babies or to give them up for adoption."

His whole body ached with a bone-deep weariness. *But she was only fifteen,* he wanted to scream until somebody heard him. She must have been scared out of her mind. Why would her parents send her to a relative?

She dragged a breath. "I would never have given her away if there was any way to keep her. You have to believe that."

"I do, Maggie." She was explaining? She was concerned about *his* feelings? He shook his head. "But you were fifteen years old. How could you take care of a baby?"

"She was *our* baby, Tony. I would have done anything."

He stroked her hair. She would have done anything, he had no doubt.

"And my parents finally agreed they'd help me raise her. But…they were on their way to be with me when—"

"Don't." He'd thought he'd heard the worst of it, but

he hadn't. He gripped her closer, needing to hold on to her. "I'm so sorry."

Her sob tore his heart. "The nurse let me hold her for a few minutes. She was so tiny…so amazing." Another sob. "She had black hair just like yours."

A chill shook him. They had a little girl somewhere in the world. *Dear God, please take care of her for us.* He kissed Maggie's hair. "Do you know where she is?"

"No. I tried to find out, but I'd signed papers agreeing her records would be sealed until she's eighteen. I don't know if she's happy or well cared for or—" Her voice broke.

He stroked her shoulders. He didn't know what to do to comfort her. He didn't know what to say. He couldn't have failed her more completely if he'd tried.

"I didn't tell anybody. Not even Jessie or Dixie. I just couldn't talk about her."

"Does Nonna know?"

She nodded. "My parents' lawyer asked her about my relatives. Stella knew I had nobody and insisted she go with him to bring me home."

"Thank God for Nonna." He hadn't even begun to understand how much he owed her. She'd taken care of him as a child. And she'd taken care of Maggie when he'd failed to do it. "Why didn't you tell me sooner?"

"I—" She shook her head. "Five years went by before we knew where you were. There was nothing you could do by then. Nothing anybody could do."

"Why didn't you tell me when I came home? Why didn't Nonna tell me?"

"She left it up to me. But you planned to stay only a few days, and I didn't want to cause you pain. I couldn't give you a reason to leave and never come back."

Is that would he would have done?

She swiped her tears from her cheeks. "I always found some reason not to tell you. But last night, I was trying to teach Hannah to tell the truth when I wasn't being honest with you. I couldn't stand myself. That's what I wanted to talk to you about later today. But when you said you were thinking about staying…I had to tell you now."

His limbs felt heavy, lifeless. His chest ached as if an elephant herd was trampling it. He'd been worried she didn't need him? She'd needed him as much as one human being could need another. And he hadn't been there for her. "How can you find it in your heart to forgive me?"

"God helped me," she said quietly.

Tony touched her soft cheek, doing his best to memorize every detail of her face. He loved her. And he wanted to be with her. But he'd hurt her beyond imagining. Would being together only cause them both more pain?

Maggie looked up at him, her eyes swollen with tears. "I'm sorry for hurting you," she said simply.

He brushed his fingers over his moist eyes and met her gaze. The pain was too fresh, too raw to deny her words. If he did, she'd know he wasn't being sincere. "None of this is your fault, Maggie. You were so young."

"So were you." She laid her head on his chest and held him close.

Leave it to Maggie to give him an out. Even when he didn't deserve it.

The sun blinding her, Maggie gulped deep breaths to try to calm herself as she hurried back to the display tent. Her heart felt like it was bleeding after leaving Tony. She couldn't seem to catch her breath.

Telling him about the baby had been even worse than she'd imagined. How would she ever forget the pain in his eyes as he grasped what she was saying and accepted responsibility for the decisions he'd made?

Now that she'd told him, everything seemed totally out of control. She had no idea what he would do. He seemed mostly…bewildered. Unable to take in everything at once. But why wouldn't he? He'd had no earthly idea what to expect when she'd told him they needed to talk.

She needed to get home to him as soon as she could.

But before she could leave, blotchy face, swollen eyes or not, she needed to face her employees manning her booths at the breakfast. She didn't have a choice. She needed them to pack up when the event was over and take care of things she'd planned to handle herself.

Thankfully, they all seemed to read her state accurately enough to keep from asking her what was wrong. And finally she got on the road, her mind torturing her all the way home about Tony and the pain and guilt she'd just dumped on him. But when she turned into the driveway, his motorcycle was gone.

She forced herself to breathe. To think. He was probably taking a long ride to sort things out. Her cell phone chirped just as she turned off the engine. Tony? She grabbed the phone and pushed the button on the way to her ear.

"Ms. McGuire?" a woman's voice asked tentatively.

"Yes." Maggie vaulted out of the truck and slammed the door.

"My name is Leona Sullivan. Laura Benson gave me your number."

Walking toward the house, Maggie let out a shaky sigh. Discussing landscaping problems was more than she could deal with right now.

"Laura showed me the rose."

"The rose?"

"The coral-pink rose with the wonderful scent."

Maggie sucked in a breath. "The Salvatore rose?"

"Yes. Laura and I are absolutely smitten with it. She knows what a rose enthusiast I am, and she thought you and I might want to discuss financial arrangements to propagate the rose."

Letting herself into the house, Maggie's head swam. Her emotions were getting in the way of sorting out appropriate questions to ask Mrs. Benson's friend.

"You haven't already found someone else to work with, have you?" the woman asked.

"No. I'm very interested in working with you. I'm sorry, I didn't get your name." *Good job, Maggie.*

"Sullivan. Leona Sullivan."

"May I get back to you as soon as I can check my schedule?"

"Of course. I'm very excited about this and am anxious to get started on the project."

Maggie did her best to summon her business voice. "I'm excited, too. Thank you so much for calling. Can I reach you at this number?"

"Yes. I look forward to your call."

Maggie clicked off her cell and laid it on the kitchen counter. Leona Sullivan could be the answer to her prayers for money for Stella's house. But right now, all she could think about was Tony.

The house seemed strangely quiet. Too quiet. An odd uneasiness creeping up her spine, she ran up the stairs and directed her steps to his room. She pushed open the door. His bed was made up so neatly, she could bounce a quarter off it. She walked to the wardrobe towering against the wall and pulled open the reluctant doors.

His things were still there.

But chills marched over her skin. He'd left his belongings behind, but she knew in her heart he was gone. His old room was empty and lonely. As empty and lonely as her life would be without him.

She walked out of the room, down the stairs, through the kitchen and out onto the back porch. Dazed, she just kept walking. Through the shadowy woods and into the bright meadow.

The hot sun did nothing to alleviate the chill deep in her bones, and she sank down near the spot of earth still blackened from his fire. She inhaled the faint odor of charred earth.

He was gone. Letting him go was part of loving him. She'd known that all along. *But it's too soon, God. I'm not ready. I didn't know I'd have to let him go so soon.*

She hugged herself, snatches of memories flitting through her mind. Tony bending over the stove, stirring one of his succulent sauces. Tony looking through old picture albums with her. Tony glistening with sweat and purpose as he pounded in the attic. And Tony holding her in the woods as she eked out the words he couldn't live with.

The sun hot on his shoulders, Tony roared through the countryside. His mind was on fire. He needed to get back to the life he could make sense of. Where things actually were as they seemed. He was desperate to get to Eau Claire where he could turn his departure over to a pilot and crew, whoever would get him out the quickest because with every fiber of his being, he wanted to stay.

He would never have believed how content he'd grown in Noah's Crossing. In Nonna's house.

With Maggie.

He glanced at his watch, an ache deep in his chest. Had she gotten home yet? Had she figured out he was gone? He should have been man enough to face her and tell her how confused and miserable he felt. That the last thing he ever wanted to do was to hurt her. That he'd hurt her enough.

Like leaving wouldn't hurt her? And without saying goodbye? What happened to his vow never to hurt her again? He braked as hard as he dared, turned onto the shoulder and stopped.

He loved Maggie. He'd always loved her. Then why was he doing exactly what he'd done at seventeen? Why was he running away?

Come to me, all you who are weary and burdened, and I will give you rest.

He shut his eyes against traffic whizzing by. He'd spent ten years trying to fill his life with new faces, new locations, new challenges. And with God's help, he'd managed to grow into a man he could respect.

But he'd made a huge mistake leaving Maggie all those years ago. A mistake that caused her more suffering than he could imagine. He'd cost them their child. It couldn't get worse than that.

So why was he running again? His dad had let the pain of loss win, over his love for his mother and his son. Was he going to let the pain win, too? Over his love for Maggie and their little girl? Was that the best he could do?

Not by a long shot.

...surviving isn't just up to us, Tony. Sometimes, resting in Him was the only way I could survive.

Sitting on his motorcycle along the highway, he gave in to the tears he'd buried inside for as long as he could remember. *I love Maggie, God. Always have. Always will. She needed me, and I wasn't there for her. Please forgive me for that. And help me forgive myself.*

He didn't know how long he sat there. Only that when he finally looked up, he felt lighter, more at peace than he'd ever felt in his life. More able to look at the future with hope. *I believe she still needs me, God. And I want to spend the rest of my life making it up to her. Please help me be the man she deserves. The man You want me to be.*

He looked for a break in traffic, then roared back onto the highway to Eau Claire. He had some serious issues to take care of.

Spent from crying, Maggie lay in the meadow watching a few clouds drift in the fathomless blue sky. She just didn't have the energy to get up and walk to the house. Nobody was there. Tony was gone. Without him, she felt as barren as the earth beside her that his fire had left behind. Another surge of tears bathed her face.

Through her tears, something glimmered in the black patch left by Tony's bonfire. Something small and green. Something new and tender and fragile. Tiny shoots poked their heads through the blackened earth. Tiny blue false indigo.

Stella had predicted the roots were deep and strong enough to sustain the plants in spite of Tony's fire.

She had deep, strong roots just like her prairie plants. And God had given her a deep, strong faith that had sustained her through everything, no matter what.

I can't possibly hold on tight enough to those I love, can I? Not my parents. Not Stella. Not our baby. And not Tony.

I must trust You to take care of them. Like You have all along. Please go on sustaining me. Please help me accept Your will and trust that in all things, You work for the good of those who love You.

"Maggie."

She could still hear Tony's voice in her head, her heart thudding in recognition. The pain of missing him was nearly unbearable.

"Maggie."

He sounded so close. So real. She felt his touch on her arm. Goose bumps danced over her skin. Her eyes flew open.

"Please don't cry." He stood looking down at her, his eyes wide-open and as vulnerable as she'd ever seen them.

Her heart picked up its cadence. Swiping her hands across her eyes, she sat upright. "You're here."

"I can't leave you," he said simply, offering his hand.

She grasped it and let him pull her to her feet beside him. She opened her mouth, but only a sob bubbled out.

Without a word, he wrapped his arms around her, pulled her to him and kissed her. Warm, secure and passionate. All she'd ever wanted in a kiss. All she'd ever needed in her life.

She flung her arms around his neck.

He stumbled back, but he recovered quickly as he lifted her off her feet.

Losing herself in the wonder of him, she clung like a climbing rose. When she ended the kiss, she leaned back to look into his eyes.

"You're part of me, Maggie. I don't know where you

leave off and I begin. I don't know how long it's been like that." His voice was hoarse with emotion. "I love you. So much I can't imagine my life without you. I don't want a life without you."

Joy exploded in her, through her, all around her. She felt as if she would burst with happiness. Tears obscuring his face, she ran her fingers through his thick hair. "I love you, too. With all that I am."

A grin relaxed his full lips and melted his eyes. He hugged her as if he'd never let her go. As if she was more precious to him than anything. Than his work. Than travel. Than freedom.

She melted against him, unable and unwilling to do anything else. He felt so strong, so secure, so solid. Her friend, her love, her life. And he was staying. Forever. In Noah's Crossing. With her.

He looked down at her. "You don't have your heart set on one of those weddings that takes months to plan, do you?"

A smile spread through her like a summer morning. "Yes, I will marry you, Tony Stefano."

He cocked his eyebrow. "Whoops. I forgot to ask." Setting her on her feet, he dropped to one knee, pulled a little box from his pocket, flipped it open and held it out to her. "Will you please marry me, Maggie McGuire?"

"It's beautiful," she breathed. "But you already have me. I can't wait to be your wife."

Standing, he slipped the sparkling solitaire diamond ring on her finger and smiled into her eyes.

She smiled back. He loved her. He wanted to marry her. She did her best to drink it all in. Still, a question nagged the edges of her mind. "You sure you'll be happy in Noah's Crossing?"

"You made me realize it's my home."

She beamed into his eyes. "Yes, it is. But...what about your project in Brazil?"

"I've been on the phone with my backers, and they agreed that our current arrangement with me consulting with my foreman is working out fine. They even agreed to build Paulo's school in exchange for several very expensive pieces of my construction equipment. They'll pay me for the rest of my equipment over time which will give us a nice piece of change to sink into that old house you and Nonna love so much."

She kissed his chin. "And I have a private backer for the Salvatore rose."

He grinned. "Fantastic. Looks like we'll be able to keep the old place from falling down and then some. So except for a vacation once in a while, I sure don't intend to drag our kids around the world. I want to raise them in that huge old house with Nonna to spoil them."

"Kids? You want kids?" Her heart beat so hard she couldn't catch her breath.

"You bet. Maybe a half dozen or so?"

"How about two or three?"

"Perfect."

Tears clouding her vision, she stretched on tiptoe and planted a kiss on his chiseled jaw. "You'll be the best dad in the whole world."

His gaze locked with hers. "Maggie, I would go back and change everything if I could. Please believe that."

She hugged him close, knowing he meant it.

He kissed her hair. "I talked with an attorney in Eau Claire who specializes in adoption cases. He agreed to try to find our little girl."

Goose bumps swarmed her body. She could hardly believe what he was saying. "He can find her? But I signed a legal document that I wouldn't try to find her until she was eighteen."

"I didn't sign it."

Maggie frowned. "I don't want to do anything that might hurt her."

"No, but we'll know if she's okay. And we can decide what to do when the time comes. Meanwhile, we have to believe God's taking good care of her."

"Yes," she whispered, her heart so full she couldn't speak. Smiling through her tears, she breathed a silent thank-you.

Epilogue

Tony lined up the unruly group in his lens for the fifth, maybe sixth, time. He'd lost count.

The light was perfect. A profusion of yellow, red, pink, white and coral roses dancing across the June-greened backyard provided the perfect backdrop. And he was going to get the perfect family picture, no matter how long it took. "Everybody say cheese on three."

"How many pictures are you planning to take?" Maggie knelt beside Nonna, who sat in a lawn chair.

"As many as it takes to get a great one." He readjusted the focus. "Ready, everybody? One, two, three."

"Cheese," they intoned, flashing the impressive smiles he wanted.

He clicked the shutter, reviewed instant replay and shook his head. "I can't see Nonna's face."

Nonna peeked out from under her big, floppy hat. "I'm trying to prevent The Terminator from getting away."

Great. What was with that kitten today? He usually lay in Nonna's lap for hours, purring like a steam engine.

Maggie reached to corral the kitten and plopped him securely in Nonna's lap alongside his well-behaved mother. Problem was, Vader took that opportunity to pounce on a leaf, the action enticing Boots to scamper away. An explosion of cats, and the chase was on.

Tony let out a breath and focused on the bright side. They could have six cats to corral instead of four if Hannah hadn't taken Whisper and Ginger to live with her. A double adoption had seemed appropriate when Maggie decided Whisper would be too lonely without a sibling to keep her company. Leave it to his wife to make sure everybody was happy.

Especially him. He'd never made a better decision in his life than to fall in love with that woman. He savored every day. She even had him involved in church stuff and loving it. Turned out, many of those people he'd been so suspicious of were his friends and neighbors.

"I'll catch them." Christa hopped up with the grace of a petite ten-year-old and raced across the lawn after the exuberant kittens, her thick, black Stefano hair blowing in the breeze. She had such a joy about her… just like Maggie.

Tears filled his eyes, remembering meeting their little girl just before Christmas. What a gift. As was the welcome her widowed adoptive mother had given them into the girl's life. Thankfully, she lived in Eau Claire which allowed frequent visits back and forth. He and Maggie couldn't be more grateful for every second they were privileged to share with their amazing child.

God was truly good.

Maggie's beautiful face alive with love, she laughed with Nonna at Christa stealthily attempting to capture the kittens. Of course, the girl and the cats had turned the whole thing into a game.

His eyes on Maggie, he lowered the camera. Looked like the perfect family picture was evading him once again. Oh, well. He had lots of imperfect ones he wouldn't give up for anything.

Seeming to sense his gaze, Maggie met his eyes, her hand fluttering to her stomach in a secret signal between them.

His heart felt like it might burst right out of his chest. They were expecting another gift next Christmas, and just last night, Maggie thought she felt their baby move for the first time. Even though she admitted it was too early and could possibly be wishful thinking.

Soon, they'd announce their news, but for now, he loved sharing their secret only with her. He took his camera from around his neck.

"Giving up on the perfect family picture for today?" Maggie asked.

"Who needs a picture?" He smiled. "I know my family by heart."

* * * * *

Dear Reader,

According to Maggie, love is not an exact science. If it was, a world-class wanderer would be the last man on earth who could still turn her into the same giddy schoolgirl she'd been when he left town ten years ago. Tony has finally come home to make things right. At least with his nonna. But as for making things right with Maggie? It's far too late for that.

Any mother can probably understand. As a mother myself, I can only imagine how heartbreaking it would be to be forced to give up a child. I know two women who found themselves in similar circumstances as Maggie when they were very young. Both women have found great joy in being reunited with their grown sons. But missing their sons' growing-up years sometimes makes their reunion bittersweet.

Although Maggie and Tony's journey eventually continues on the bumpy road to love, they have some pretty big bumps to navigate, among them forgiveness and self-acceptance. I hope you find inspiration in their struggle to overcome past disappointments and abandonments and to turn to God to help them forgive themselves and each other.

I hope *Instant Daddy* readers who asked for Maggie's story are pleased to find out what happened to her. As always, I'd love to hear your thoughts and feelings about the book. You can write to me at Love Inspired Books, 233 Broadway, Suite 1001, New York, NY 10279, or email me at carol@carolvoss.com or visit me on the web at www.carolvoss.com.

Grace always,
Carol Voss

Questions for Discussion

1. Tony heads home because he needs forgiveness. Have you ever needed forgiveness? Did you ask for it? Did you receive forgiveness or not? How did you feel about the outcome?

2. Given Maggie's situation when she was fifteen, could she have made a different decision than to give her baby up for adoption? What would you have done?

3. Tony and his nonna have conflicting views of Tony's father. Why? Whose view do you identify with? Why?

4. Tony's father left when Tony was six years old. Do you think his father's actions still drive Tony? If so, how?

5. Given Maggie's history, can you understand her desire to hang on to people and things in her life? Why or why not?

6. Do you agree with Maggie that Tony abandoned her when she needed him most? If so, would you be able to forgive him? How is Maggie able to do it?

7. How do you think Maggie was able to overcome her losses and build the life she has?

8. Maggie struggles to find God's plan for her life. Can you see God's hand in your own life? Can you

identify times He has somehow changed the course you've been following?

9. Tony says he prefers to worship in God's great outdoors. Can you understand why he feels that way? Why or why not?

10. Tony and Maggie have both experienced deep disappointments in their lives, yet Tony admits Maggie has more faith in people than he does. Do you agree with him? Why or why not?

11. At fifteen, Maggie made a decision that changed her life forever. Have you or a loved one ever made a decision that changed your life? Perhaps when you were very young? If not, do you know someone who experienced this? How have you or someone you know dealt with it?

12. Maggie is certain Stella will not get well if she cannot come home to her beloved garden and old Victorian. Do you agree with Maggie? Or do you think Tony is right in his belief that his nonna will be relieved if she doesn't have the worries associated with the old house? Why?

13. Do you understand Hannah's decision to disobey the rules? Have you ever felt that taking a risk was worth the consequences? Was it? Why or why not?

14. "For if you forgive men when they sin against you, your heavenly Father will also forgive you." —*Matthew* 6:14. Have you ever had trouble living by these powerful words? Why or why not?

INSPIRATIONAL

Love Inspired

COMING NEXT MONTH
AVAILABLE APRIL 24, 2012

MONTANA HOMECOMING
The McKaslin Clan
Jillian Hart

BUILDING A PERFECT MATCH
Chatam House
Arlene James

LEAH'S CHOICE
Hannah's Daughters
Emma Miller

THE BULL RIDER'S BABY
Cooper Creek
Brenda Minton

HER SMALL-TOWN SHERIFF
Moonlight Cove
Lissa Manley

HOMETOWN FAMILY
Mia Ross

Look for these and other Love Inspired books wherever books
are sold, including most bookstores, supermarkets, discount
stores and drugstores.

LICNM0412